Pia Lera

Secret of the Beaded Belt

An adventure through the
grasslands discovering wildlife

Illustrated by Milena Riley

DEDICATION

To my grandchildren Sabrina, Paolo, Isabella and Giulia
who are my inspiration and their mothers who have
given me so much. To all the children that I taught,
remember that learning should be fun and a pleasure to
be treasured. To all the children in the family, young and
old, this is for you too. Help conserve this wonderful
heritage of wild animals that has been left in your trust.

ACKNOWLEDGMENTS

To write a book is a very lonely enterprise. It cannot be done without the help of friends and family who give of their time, emotions and comments. I could not have finished the book without Milena's honest comments, who also provided the images. Thank you for sharing my journey.

To Gwynneth, Di, Sheila, Denny, and Mary Jane who read the manuscript and gave their comments through their teacher eyes, thank you for your friendship. To Peter, who gave me an insight into writing for a young reader, you have my admiration. To Audrey who shared her unlimited expertise in children's books, I appreciate your guidance. James, you are the monkey in the tree. Piero who patiently waited for the book to be finished, you are my rock.

CONTENTS

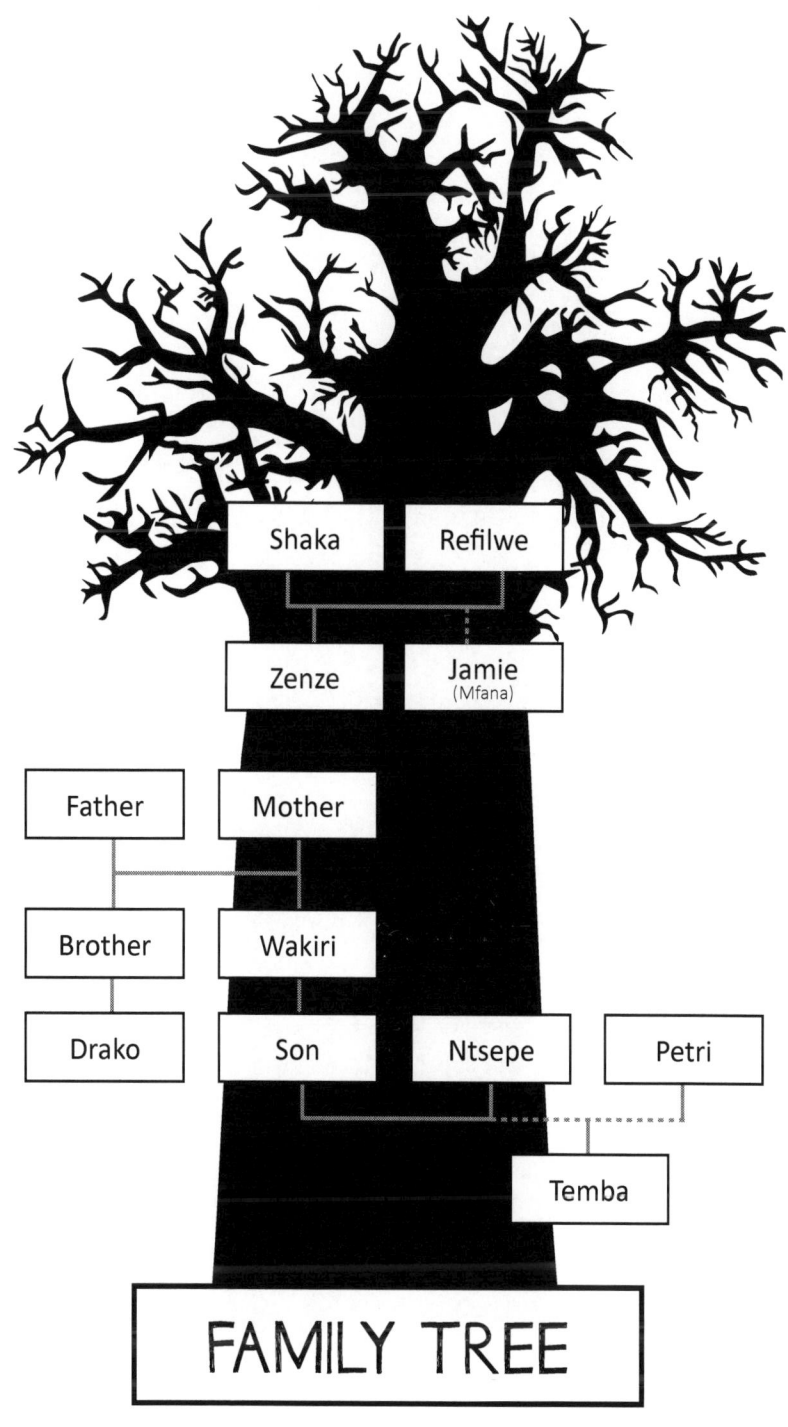

Shaka | Refilwe

Zenze | Jamie
(Mfana)

Father | Mother

Brother | Wakiri

Drako | Son | Ntsepe | Petri

Temba

FAMILY TREE

CHAPTER I
>>>><<<<

....they became inseparable...

omewhere in Africa, the sun is rising and Jamie, (called Mfana, 'little boy') hears the sounds of the forest as he reluctantly becomes aware that it is time to wake up. He hears the swish-swish of his mother's short broom as she sweeps around the mud hut and the smell of burning wood alerts his tummy that mielie meal (soft corn porridge) is cooking in the black pot hanging over the fire and breakfast is ready. He is content. He does not need to open his eyes to know that he is not alone, he can feel the added warmth of Xixi his pet *monkey* on his back. He opens one eye and then the other and a mischievous smile curls the ends of his mouth. He wonders whether today he will be able to creep from under his

1

blankets without waking the black-faced, long-tailed monkey. A game they have played ever since Xixi was newborn. Jamie's earliest memories are intertwined with this ball of fur nestling in his neck. He remembers waking up and not knowing where he was, afraid at being alone and being cared for by dark-skinned people who were completely different from himself. He remembers not understanding their language but seeing kindness in their eyes. He remembers the softness of Refilwe's skin, his brown mother, as she held him in her arms. He will never forget the little monkey that was placed in his arms, so small it felt as if he was holding air. Enormous eyes looked at him from its furry face, with tears hanging in the corners. Tiny hands clenched each other and its body language showed hopelessness and sorrow. "He too has lost his mother," said Zenze his brown brother. "He too needs someone to look after him and love him. Look after him well and he will become your friend for life." Jamie cradled the little monkey and fell in love with it right away, nuzzling him while the monkey made little 'xixi' noises. "Your name will be Xixi and I will look after you forever." From that day onwards, they were inseparable, each one looking after the other, their mutual need filling the empty gap in their lives.

Jamie hears bleating and a 'hrmph, hrmph' sound that he identifies as Zenze milking the goats for breakfast milk. He thinks of Zenze and mentally strokes his peppercorn hair to tell him just how much he loves him. He knows it was Zenze who saved his life.

Jamie occasionally has flashback images that appear and disappear in an instant, similar to the shutter on a camera, where he sees a lady with golden hair and blue eyes hugging him close and twirling him in her arms. At these times when the images disappear, he recalls a perfume on the fringes of his memory, a smell he cannot place, making him feel happy and tranquil. Often, while walking in the forest he stops and sniffs the air and in the blink of an eye, he thinks he can recall that perfume but he is always disappointed as it dissipates into thin air, forever etched in his memory. Sometimes he remembers riding on the shoulders of a big man, but the memories are short-lived and fade quickly. Many times he asks Zenze to repeat the story of how he saved him, over and over, taking in the details for later recall. He has a thirst to know every detail. He knows there are answers for him just out of his reach, just out of sight. He is different, his hair is white and straight, his eyes are green, while everyone else's are dark black and their hair very curly.

His skin is much paler than Zenze's, and becomes red and sore if he stays in the sun too long. He is the same color all over, while all his family is dark brown with pink palms and soles. Refilwe, to protect his legs from the sun, has fashioned long pants for him instead of the loin cloth the other boys wear and even though his skin from the waist up is exposed to the sun and has a brownish tan, he needs to wear a shirt made from hide to protect his body.

Refilwe, is the most beautiful person in the world to this nine year old boy. Just thinking of her makes him feel happy. When he snuggles in her lap, he thinks of it as a Chief's throne, so comfortable and safe so that no one and nothing can harm him while he is in his mother's lap. Even now that he is a big boy, he loves to have the odd cuddle in her lap. He thinks that mothers are the best people in the world. She smells of smoke and cooking and after a wash in the river she smells like the earth's first smell of dew, kissed by the early morning sunrays, a smell unique to Africa that once experienced is carved into the senses forever.

He becomes aware of other sounds – he hears the chickens clucking and imagines them pecking in the red dust for insects or bits of corn thrown out for them. He hears laughing and babies crying and knows who these

4

sounds belong to. That baby crying is Mogadi – she was born just a few nights ago and cries a lot. That cough belongs to Nano who has come home to be looked after by his family. He worked in the mines for many years and caught the mine-sickness that made many men sick.

Jamie knows everyone in the kraal (village) and feels content and secure. The hut he lives in forms part of the Chief's compound in the middle of the kraal, with all the other huts in a circle around it. He is welcomed into any hut at any time. There are no doors and the windows are openings covered with animal hides. He hears the long-tailed, grey loerie birds making loud noises as they chase each other from branch to branch in a follow-my-leader manner. Kay-waaay, kay-waaay they call to each other. He pictures them bathing in the little rock pool he and Zenze made for the birds under the mopani tree. They splash and wash themselves noisily, one loerie always on the lookout while the others bathe. That hum in his ears, he knows, are the 'miggies' the tiny flying insects that fly in swarms and often into ones mouth and nose – harmless but annoying. He smiles as he thinks of the 'miggie dance', so named by him when he or his friends try to wave these insects away. When the miggies 'attack' they leave no exposed skin unaffected and to get rid of them one has to flail arms, legs and shake ones head while trying to keep your mouth closed. Many a time through laughing at the antics of a friend, Jamie swallowed a few miggies to the delight of all and coughed and spluttered until he spewed them out.

Jamie springs out of bed like an arrow shouting "Aiee, Aiee" as he feels little monkey hands around his neck, stuck to him like a leech – even today he has not been able to trick Xixi. Jamie rolls up his blanket and tucks it into the beam of the roof. He struggles into his shirt and moves towards the opening of the hut, drawing back the hard cow hide covering. The fresh air hits his lungs like a song hits the brain, and immediately he takes in deep, slow breaths, stretches his limbs and gives his eyes a good old rub. He scratches his arms and the back of his thighs and feels the already warm earth beneath his soles. His world has not changed, everything is as he left it last night and yet Jamie is experiencing strange sensations as 'old' memories, the ones before he came to this home are beginning to 'jump out at him' at the most unexpected times.

"Greetings my son, did you travel easily in your dreams?"

"Greetings mother, yes I dreamt things that I have

already forgotten, as always. I do remember though, that the golden lady came to visit me again and smiled at me. She looked happy. My tummy is rumbling like a hungry lion. Zenze, big brother, come and eat with me – I know you have fresh goat's milk for me, I heard you saying sweet words to our goat so she would give you the best milk for me."

"Your ears are too big for such a small boy, you hear things you should not be hearing. Why should such a puny, pale person be so special to me that I would wake up before the sun shows her face over the hills to milk the goats?"

"You know that I am your gift from the sky, you told me so yourself."

"Aieesh," but you are getting too cheeky for your head, soon you will be ready for the 'making-of-a-man school."

The bantering went on while they sat on a log eating porridge out of hollowed-out gourds, with their hands. Xixi too was eating porridge from a gourd with his little paw, wiping his eyes and mouth after each mouthful. Refilwe poured milk into the gourds and the boys slurped loudly as they ate and talked about the day's happenings.

"Zenze, I am afraid of the making-of-a-man-school.

My friend Leto went away and only his dead body came back. I saw his mother crying and wailing and his father looked with dull eyes on the body. Why must boys go away to that fearful school? Why won't anybody tell me? I don't want you to go and I certainly don't want to go. You are older than me and I have heard mutterings that soon it will be time for you to go. Please, please don't go, I am afraid." Zenze looks at Jamie with a resigned look and shaking his head says, "it is the way of our people , but I will tell you a secret – I too am afraid, very afraid."

Jamie is aware that Temba, his 'girl cousin', is out and about as he had caught a glimpse of her down at the river bending down to collect water for the day. It was the girls who fetched water for the whole household and sometimes she would complain. "Aiee! but water can be so heavy – I wonder how something that you can see through can be so heavy." Just then, he sees her walking through the tall veld grass with a clay bowl on her head and at this distance could even see the droplets shooting out of the bowl, caught in the sun and shining like crystals before disappearing into the grass. The grass is so tall that she looks as if she has no body, only her head and bowl visible. He laughs and points.

"Look at Temba, she is a floating head – the Tokoloshe

must have taken the rest of her body."

"Don't laugh about the Tokoloshe, my son, it can be evil and spiteful," scolded Refilwe, "you had better go and throw some of your porridge into the river to appease it."

"The Tokoloshe does not frighten me – he is afraid of my pale skin and besides I am taller than him, in fact I am going to call him Tiki, then he will have no power over me. Xixi, you will protect me, won't you?" Xixi at the sound of his name looks up and seeing Temba jumps up and down making monkey noises, 'xi, xi, xi', thumping his tummy, twirling around in a show of joy.

"Don't be silly," snapped Refilwe, "you never know when he is watching skinny, white boys."

Jamie gets up and gives a mock dance, lifting his arms and legs in a warrior dance, singing.

" Tiki, Tiki, the ugly One

Show yourself and I'll run and I'll run"

Just then, a wild wind rushes through the tall grass shaking the reeds in the river, scaring the ducks roosting in their depths. They take off with wings flapping, touching the water, causing ripples on the previously calm surface, accompanied by their 'quaa, quaa' sounds. The household dogs whine and slink towards the huts and the fire burning under the porridge pot splutters and dies. Temba suddenly trips and the water bowl topples off her head and smashes into the mud. She stamps her feet in anger because now she has to go back to the river and fetch more water. She shakes her arms and then re-arranges the beaded belt around her waist, the belt she wears every day.

Refilwe shakes all over and picking up hot porridge from Jamie's bowl, rushes to the river bank and throws bits into it, intoning: "Tokoloshe, Great One, take no heed of this strange son of mine, he is different and does not know what he is saying. He is only a cheeky boy, with no respect for a spirit as great as you. Accept this offering from the very bowl from which he has eaten and forgive him his rudeness." She turns around and gives Jamie her "snake eyes look", that says 'don't do that again!' It's a known fact that mothers all over the world give their children *that* look.

Jamie laughs and slaps his pants, pointing to Refilwe and mimics her snake eyes, but a shiver of fear makes him tighten his muscles from his neck to his waist and he thinks: If the Tiki really existed, surely he would have shown himself by now?

This morning, for some reason unknown to himself, Jamie watched Temba with interest. Temba was his 'little mother'. She was five years older than him and had helped to take care of him as a baby. She too had carried him on her back and sung to him.

"Little sunshine on my back

You're so pale and I'm so brown

You're my brother, like no other,

Little Ilanga (sun) you are mine."

She looked different to him today, she looked older, sadder, more grown up than he could remember. He suddenly felt as if his world was tilting a little and that great changes were about to happen.

CHAPTER 2

....the forest has ears...

Jamie's sleeping arrangements until recently had been flexible. He slept either with his mother or Temba, but now that she was getting ready to be married, she slept on her own blanket by herself. There was change in the air this morning, it felt as if time was suspended or the feeling that something very different was going to happen. As Temba had walked towards them with the bowl of water on her head, Jamie noticed an unhappiness about her. She was usually the cheekiest of the trio and her smile the widest, but this morning her gaze was far away and her walk did not have a spring to it, it seemed she had the worries of the world on her shoulders. He noticed her hips swaying, they were fuller than he remembered; he noticed her breasts were beginning to show and he knew, because he had seen her when they were swimming, that soft hairs grew in her private place and under her arms.

He kept checking his own body but none of these signs were visible – yet. He had asked Zenze about this and he had said, "when the time is right your body will change as well – it is nature's way."

"Have you eaten, Temba? Do you want some of my porridge and milk? Zenze specially milked the goat for us."

"No, I don't feel like eating today."

"Let's go and find some marogo for our mother so she can cook it for supper."

"Somehow, I don't even feel like that even though it is my favorite food. You go and find the marogo, but remember, be sure you pick only the lovely new leaves, the dark green leaves taste bitter."

"Oh! Come on Temba, what's the matter with you? We can go for a swim afterwards to clean off all the dirt from our hands and feet."

"You are a pest! I suppose I'll have to go with you, otherwise you'll buzz around me the whole morning, like a mosquito looking for my blood! I'll go with you, if you promise to help me fetch water, later on."

"Go with him Temba, enjoy your last times with him," said Refilwe.

"What last times, what does she mean, where are

you going? Tell me." Panic seized him in the pit of his stomach, making him feel sick. "What are you not telling me? What is the secret you are not telling me?"

"Okay, nosey one, let's go – I'll tell you on the way," she replied with a subdued voice.

"Where are you two going"? boomed a loud voice from the shade of the flame tree. "Have you done your chores? Who is going to bring me tobacco for my pipe? I have to see to all the problems of my kraal while you two go off wandering into the forest. Who is going to bring me water to wash my hands and feet after hours of listening to the moans and groans of my people. Do you think it is easy being Chief?" Jamie ran to Shaka his father, stood before him and inclined his head, touching the left side over his heart with the palm of his right hand and then touching his father over his heart, softly with great respect.

"Morning father, I did not see you here in the shade. It is such a lovely morning, we are going to pick some *marogo* (wild spinach) for your supper. We'll try and find some marula fruit for you as well, if the elephants have not eaten them all, you know how they love that fruit." Jamie knew it was custom to respect one's father and in the case of his father the Chief, praise was expected. "We all know that you work so hard at looking after the people in the kraal and we love and respect you for that. We will not be long. We'll soon be back to bring you whatever you need."

"There are snakes out there, not only the reptile kind. There are evil people who will try to lead you astray, so be careful, my children. Respect Nature and do not harm the earth". Jamie looked fondly at his father, this thin, white haired man who taught him so much.

"My precious children, said Shaka, let me give you a blessing before you go, to protect you against the outside world. Standing opposite him with heads bowed, he held his hands over their heads and intoned: "Great Spirit of the skies, look after my children, protect them from the dangers of the world. Keep them safe from scorpions at their feet and leopards in the trees and everything in between because they have few brains and talk and talk without looking around for danger. They do not hear the rustling in the reeds or the stealthy sound of leaves being crushed; they are unaware of the smells of danger. I let them go only because they will be under Your protection."

He made his voice boom, but the corners of his mouth curled up at the thought that maybe they had not listened to a word. Jamie and Temba had often heard variations

15

of this blessing and joyfully set off into the African bush. Shaka's wisdom was sought after and people flocked to hear him speak. A fair Chief and leader, giving every problem his complete attention. He knew everyone and their ancestors and could trace his lineage to the great chief Shaka Zulu. He led by example and never advised violence to resolve problems. Hand in hand, Temba, balancing a basket on her head and Jamie carrying a spear and a leather pouch around his waist with Xixi on his shoulder, made their way towards the river bank.

Refilwe anxiously scanned the farthest bank for crocodiles who basked in the sun for most of the day, soaking up much needed warmth for when they wallow in the water. A crocodile, silent and deadly will take its prey in its mouth and carry it to his cave underwater, leaving it to rot until ready to be eaten. Every year people disappeared from the kraal after fetching water or washing in the river. Refilwe spat three times into the earth as a gesture of protection towards her children. Oh, how she worried about her children's safety.

The old chief leaned on his spear listening carefully in the direction of the two children and monkey disappearing from the kraal. He could not look directly into Refilwe's eyes but he felt that she was sad. "Come and sit with me Refilwe, I feel you are troubled, as am I. Bring me a gourd of your special drink, skokiaan, and let's talk." They sat on a log under the flame tree, the occasional bright red petal falling onto them. The repetitive buzz of the bees, busily moving from blossom to blossom created a soothing background and the Chief spoke.

"We are nearing a time of change in our family – I can feel it. I heard the mousebirds – the ones with the very red face and black beaks calling to each other 'too weewee, too weeweewee' before sunrise and a *shongololo* worm  with its hundred little legs crawled over my feet at full moon – all signs that change is in the air. I know that you are not happy that Temba has been promised to Drako. I know that you and Zenze do not like him. You have been a good mother to her, but her true mother, Ntsepe, is not here to make decisions for her and it is our custom to not refuse a chief's wishes. Chief Wakiri is a powerful man and Temba will be welcomed into such an important family. Why are you not happy about this marriage?"

"Drako is an arrogant young man, who is cruel to animals, killing them for sport and not for the pot. He has a spear that spits fire and no animal or man is safe from him," she whispered in a shaky voice. "I hear that he stole it from the white men at the camp. Our Temba's heart will shatter were she to marry such a man. She is kind and generous and loves animals but most of all she is so young – what does she know of life? She is happy here with us. Why must she leave us and marry a stranger, especially Drako? My heart is breaking at the thought. I wish her mother Ntsepe were here to make the decision. I love Temba as if she were my own and not my sister's child. Drako is only interested in her beauty not her heart. I am afraid for Temba."

Refilwe paused for a few moments, wiping her eyes, and continued. "At night when I travel to the other world in my dreams I see my sister crying and pleading with me to protect her child. She asks me to be wary of Chief Wakiri because he is influenced by that Witchdoctor Horrifendi.

"Hush, my wife, the forest has ears and Horrifendi's reach is endless." Refilwe leans towards her husband and in a whisper says, "Horrifendi is a creepy leech that sucks the life out of people. His eyes bulge like a bullfrog's and his breath smells like a rhino midden. He is evil, evil, evil." Refilwe hugged herself and shivered. "I fear that when Temba leaves us, we will never see her again, her husband will forbid it because Horrifendi will have twisted his thoughts with muti (medicine). I have heard that Horrifendi roams the forest at night, looking for poisonous mushrooms and digging for dangerous roots. He then makes a magical, poisonous brew that stinks and bubbles without heat. I think he is an evil creature in man's clothing – I'm sure his blood is green and slimy."

"Shhhhhhh! my wife, do not say these things. Let's smoke a pipe and think on it, maybe, if Temba could speak to her mother, Ntsepe might be able to help her change Chief Wakiri's mind."

"How is that possible, my sister lives in a hidden kraal, surrounded by high mountains, and the entrance a fiercely guarded secret. I have heard tales that specially trained hadidah birds (black Ibis), give off their loud squawks, 'kwaa, kwaa, kwaa,' and alert the guards. Those birds give me the shivers, they are scary looking, so large and noisy and their droppings are huge and messy."

"I heard that two-headed crocodiles protect the river surrounding the kraal," said Shaka, sucking air through the gaps in his teeth where the rotten ones had fallen out. Did he have the slightest tilt to his lips as he said this? Was he enjoying teasing his wife?

"Please stop, I cannot bear to listen one more

moment," cried Refilwe as goose pimples popped up all over her body.

Sucking on his pipe, a little dribble collecting in the corner of his mouth, Shaka observed. "Not only do we have the sadness of Temba, but what about Mfana? He is growing up so quickly and asking questions about his early life more often. He is also beginning to remember his previous life. We soon will have to tell him everything we know and help him make decisions." Refilwe stood up, shook her skirt, shuffled her feet a few times in the red dust, and looking down whispered, "my heart is so heavy, I need to do something with my hands. I am going to pound some corn so I can have thick porridge ready for the children when they get back. When I am busy I can think clearly. I also want to try my new oven in that anthill at the back of the kraal. Wait for me at the oven, I am going to collect some iron wood."

Unbeknown to the Chief and his wife, every word they said had been overheard by Zenze who had returned home early from herding the goats. One of the kids had a festering sore on its leg and he wanted some of Refilwe's medicine to keep the wound clean. He had seen his parents sitting under the flame tree and as most children do, loved to overhear conversations, he learnt a lot at these times! While he crouched behind a thorn bush, known as the *'wag-'n-bietjie'* (wait-a-while) bush, careful not to get too close, he heard the anguish in their voices and felt their troubled hearts.

How could he tell them that he too had a heavy heart and did not know what to do about it. He too had a problem. He knew his initiation, the making-of-a-man time was near but he was not happy about it at all. He knew that if he did not go through with it, his parents would be shamed and they would become the laughing stock of the tribe. His ancestors would bring bad luck onto the kraal. How could he tell them that he, the chief's son was afraid?"

CHAPTER 3

....he feels a furry little body...

emba loves the feel of Mfana's little plump hand in hers. How could she ever explain the customs and traditions of her tribe to this little stranger, yet brother? How is she going to tell him that she is leaving soon to be the unhappy bride of someone she does not love and is afraid of? She does not have the choice to disagree with this arrangement. She feels such a wave of protection towards Jamie that she crushes his small hand in hers.

"Aiee, Aiee what is the matter, what have I done! Why are you hurting me?"

She bends down immediately and kisses his hand. "I'm sorry, I'm sorry, my little Llanga, my sun, I didn't mean to hurt you, I was just thinking of something scary and my thoughts ran away from me, that's why I clutched your hand so hard."

"Girls!" says Jamie, rolling his eyes.

"What do you know about girls?" says Temba, with a smile.

"My friend Nelson says girls always have their heads in the clouds – always thinking about boys, always giggling and acting silly."

She makes a playful attempt at punching him on the arm, but he is too quick and runs away, Xixi hanging on for dear life! "What does Nelson know, he is but a child himself, although I must admit that he says some wise things, for his age!" She turns away from him so he cannot see her tongue pushing against her inner cheek and her smiley eyes. She is very fond of Nelson, the peacemaker in the children's circle. He is always the one leading by good example, breaking up fights and making up fun games with everyone. He is not a 'woer-woer', a tornado like Jamie, but a sensible, maybe too serious a child for his age, although his remark about 'girls' has made her chuckle – maybe he is not as serious as she thought! She knows that he will be a great leader of men when he grows up.

Their path takes them along the river bank, near enough to see the dragonflies darting onto the surface of the water, causing circular ripples, the ever present frogs eyeing them for a future treat, and the occasional

 *dragon fly* disappearing underwater into the jaws of a greedy fish. Temba peers intently on the river surface, checking to see whether any hippos are close to the river bank. She knows hippos are very dangerous, especially when they are feeding or have young ones in tow. The best course of action is to move away as quickly as possible, so she subconsciously tracks a getaway path, keeping in mind that hippos are as happy on land as they are in water.

She casually skims the surface of the water looking for crocodiles, Jamie follows her gaze and says, "I have already looked for the 'log-with-eyes', and there don't seem to be any around at the moment, but let's not walk too near the riverbank – you know how fast they are on land, swishing their long tails and running on those short, stumpy legs! It gives me the creeps, but at the same time I find crocs very funny, with their eyes and nostrils the only part of their enormous, scaly body showing above the water surface. No wonder they can float noiselessly and stay in the water for a long time. Temba, have you seen how crocodiles lie on the sandy bank of the river with their jaws open?"

"Ugh! Yuck! the inside of their mouths is yellow and those teeth! No way do I ever want to get too close to those! And how does a *crocodile* allow those little birds to clean in between their teeth without eating them?" Temba starts singing:

> 'Gliding soundlessly in the lakes
>
> No one knows what sound he makes
>
> His eyes so evil, so tough his skin
>
> You'd be tasty, even though you are so thin!'

Jamie puts his elbows together clapping his hands as if it were a crocodile's mouth, weaving around Temba and making crunching noises at her legs. "I'm a hungry crocodile, let me taste your legs". She playfully shoos him away, kicking her legs backwards.

The path has been well trodden and muddy so they follow the drier smaller paths made by many feet, away from the wet parts. They are careful of where they place their feet. A branch with thorns across the path means that someone who has walked the path before is pointing

25

to a thorn bush or a hidden hole in the path. A large stone placed right in the middle means 'look for signs'. Temba points and exclaims, "look, *Mfana* (little boy), see the drag line in the sand? A snake, not a very big one, has slithered here, and quite recently, as the marks are distinct, were they old, the wind would have swept them away.

"How do we know the snake is not close by, ready to strike?"

"I don't know for certain, but snakes are more afraid of us than we are of them," she says laughingly, "they can feel the vibrations of something coming close to them, 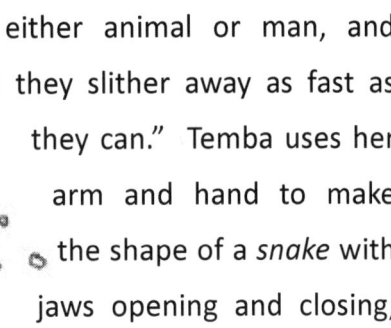either animal or man, and they slither away as fast as they can." Temba uses her arm and hand to make the shape of a *snake* with jaws opening and closing, swaying in the air, stalking Jamie, saying...

"Sssssss I'm a slithering snake,

no matter how quiet,

I can hear every noise you make ...Sssssss".

Jamie laughs and makes hissing sounds back. Their antics have disturbed a ringed plover who stalks away from them on its long pale yellow-orange legs, trying to move them away from a well hidden nest in the grass, softly calling 'tooee, tooee'.

"Don't worry plover bird, we are not looking for your nest to steal your eggs, stop making such a noise!" the bird is so outraged that it flies very close over their heads, trying to head them away from its nest.

Temba and Jamie walk together, at times in single file at times hand in hand, while Xixi takes the opportunity to climb up trees and swing from one branch to the other chattering "xi, xi" all the time. When he strays out of sight, Jamie makes a clicking sound with his tongue that brings him back immediately. They take a path that leads towards a well known thicket of trees. They skirt it to approach the fields where the marogo grows. He knows this plant well. It took him a long time to like the taste, but now just thinking about it makes his mouth water. Being a young boy, he is always thinking of food.

Marogo grows wild in places that are a well guarded secret. The villagers know that it could mean the difference between starvation and life, and when the rainy season is late or the corn fields have been depleted, it is this leaf similar to spinach that sustains them. Temba knows to pick just enough for the family as she has been taught that no food should ever be wasted. She picks a little more to be given to the old couple who live under the fever tree. Old Madala and his wife Gogo are looked after and respected by the whole kraal. It is an unwritten law that old parents are shared and villagers take it in turn to see to their needs.

Temba and Jamie hear the gurgling of the stream even before they see it, and parting the high green grass walk towards its bank. As they walk towards the stream, Temba says, "listen carefully, the river ladies are rustling their skirts, that is the sound you hear."

"Don't be silly, Temba, that's the sound of the Tiki running after the ladies," he teases.

"What am I going to do with you, wicked one, you have no respect for the Tokoloshe, and I am afraid that one day he is going to do you harm."

Jamie laughed, "I've told you, I'm not afraid of the Tiki – he is afraid of my pale skin and green eyes." Just then, the sound of crackling, dry grass, buffeted by a strong wind becomes louder and circles them, the sound reaches such a pitch that it leaves them unmoving. A burst of dust belts into Jamie's eyes making him rub them. Eyes darting from left to right, Temba tries to find out where the sound is coming from but she is disoriented and very afraid. Xixi hangs onto Jamie's leg and chatters his teeth as if he were cold, covering his eyes with a hand. Temba shivers and holds Jamie's hand tightly. "How can we hear the sound of dry grass crackling, when all around us the grass is green. Could it be the Tokoloshe?" gasps Temba.

"Don't be such a fraidy girl, it was all in your imagination, it was just a gust of wind." Jamie does not want to admit it, but he is feeling anxious and wary too, "lets pick the marogo quickly so we can go and have a swim – it's so hot already."

Xixi is nowhere to be seen, having run away at the strange sound. Jamie clicks his tongue a few times and he reappears, jumping up and down on the branch of a tree, screeching 'xi,xi,xi.' He is terrified, and Jamie has to coax him down into his arms, by offering him some pumpkin seeds from his left pocket. He feels in his right pocket and is reassured when he feels a furry little body. What they do not see are two red, yellow-centred, flashy eyes, with green slimy gung collected in the corners. A fine, foul smelling mist squirted from these eyes, causing the foliage it touched to wilt immediately. A rotten, disgusting stench lingered in the still air. They approach the muddy, slippery bank of the cool stream. Standing in the clear water up to her ankles, Temba tucks her skirt into her underwear and facing the bank, starts collecting the wild spinach leaves and places them in her basket. Jamie plays around a little, splashing her and kicking the water, picking up a stone and throwing it at an unseen target. He finds a stick and watches it float down the stream, helping it around the boulders. A lizard darts out from behind a stone and curls its tongue around an unsuspecting bug, then motionlessly lies in the sun, on the lookout for another tasty morsel. A glossy starling chirps from a nearby tree, 'trrr-chree-chrrr' its yellow-orange eyes staring while the sun plays games on its feathers, one moment blue and the other green. Xixi washes his face, jumping up and down and scooting around in circles, squealing at Jamie's splashes. Jamie tries to splash Xixi as much as he can, because he knows he has fleas and a good soaking would do his fur a lot of good. He has watched other *monkeys* groom each other, and knows that he needs to do this for Xixi, if he is to remain healthy. His father explained that in a troupe of monkeys, many friendly hours are spent looking for and killing fleas from each other's fur. It is a way of making friends and meeting other monkeys. Jamie knows that it is important to control the fleas because the bite of a flea leaves a little wound that can become infected if not kept clean. Just as body hygiene is necessary for humans to stay healthy, so is it necessary for animals. Jamie often complains, as boys do, that it is not necessary to bathe regularly, keep ones hands clean, brush teeth and keep ones room tidy, but his mom Refilwe is strict about the rules of hygiene. She sees that he cleans his teeth with the cold ashes from the family fire and that he bathes in the safe part of the river with her special soap made from hippo fat.

Animals, and humans, learn from their parents, mostly their mothers, how to clean themselves, but Xixi has been hand-reared by Jamie who has had to learn how to be his mother. Sometimes, Xixi plays with friendly monkeys, learning many tricks from them and the occasional one has groomed him, but he is not always welcome into a troupe. The monkeys can smell the human scent on him and will not accept him easily into their family. Xixi has learnt to make himself understood by grinning, smacking his lips and yawning to show off his large canine teeth that are sharp and deadly. Yawning is a known aggressive

31

gesture in the animal world.

While looking for fleas in Xixi's fur, Jamie wonders about his own real parents. Did his real mother groom him? Did she hug him like he hugs Xixi? Did she smell like Refilwe? What about his father? He has lost his memory but occasionally a thought, an idea, or a new word creeps into his memory making him wonder about his life before now. He is becoming aware of another time in his life, he just cannot wrap his mind around it.

CHAPTER 4

.....She notices a piece of string......

emba has picked the wild spinach steadily, with a soft smile playing around her lips. She is well aware that Jamie is not helping, but enjoying himself with Xixi in the water. She will miss this little brother who holds her heart. He came to them so suddenly, so injured and she worries about how he will manage without her, how he will reach manhood in an honorable, safe manner. She touches the beaded necklace around her neck and says a silent prayer to Mother Earth to look after him and to protect him from the evil spirits, especially Tiki. She makes a mental note to make a beaded necklace for Jamie to ward off evil spirits. Her own mother made a necklace for her and she has never taken it off – she is sure it has kept her safe all these years. She also makes sure that the belt around her waist is secure.

Casting her eyes up into the sky, she hears rustling

in the nearest tree and knows, without looking, that it's the two *loeries* that follow Mfana all the time. Their call has followed them since they left the kraal. She has known they were there for a while now, but has said nothing. These large grey birds are loving birds and easily tamed and for some reason have taken a liking to Jamie, of course, the fruit he leaves out for them every day could be one of the reasons. Smiling inwardly, she wants to believe that because of their distinctive cry 'goway, goway' they are chasing evil away from Jamie, her llanga – her sun.

"Come on Jamie, picker-of-no-use, I have done all the work while you have been playing. Let's move out of the sun." Basket on her head, Temba makes her way towards the thicket of trees with Jamie, while Xixi trails behind. "Look," she exclaims, a little *duiker* has come this way you can see his small droppings and they are still quite fresh, so he is not

34

far away." Bending down, she points to a broken twig. "He must have enjoyed a little meal here, see where his teeth ripped the leaves? I can see his hoof prints in the dust, there are smaller ones too, there must have been a baby as well." Temba squats low, close to the prints and exclaims, "this little duiker was alarmed because I can see that it 'froze' in its tracks and leaned forward – see how the hoof prints are deeper at the front? – that is typical of what a duiker does when it stops and is afraid of danger. If you look sharply, you can tell exactly what happened. The clues nature leaves us, tell a story."

"All you have to do is *be aware and look around you*," mimics Jamie. He squints his eyes playfully at Temba, because these are the words she and Zenze continually use when out in the wild with him. Taking a right turn, they amble down a twisty path towards the clump of trees.

It takes a few seconds for their eyes to adjust to the cool shadows of the wood. They have entered through a tunnel-like entrance with heavy branches low down near the ground. Immediately they are surrounded by changing light as if they were looking up at the surface of a pool from underwater. In a blink it is like another world, the hot, bright, clear vista has been replaced by a shadowy, cool, humid atmosphere. 'Goway, goway' call the two loerie birds, landing on the odd branch, chasing each other in a game. Although well trodden, the path is narrow, littered with fallen leaves and pods. Temba and Jamie walk around rocks, tendrils and low lying branches carefully. With heightened senses they keep their gaze lowered because anyone who has lived in Africa knows, there could be danger behind any bush and a hidden tendril could cause a bad fall, or not be a tendril at all but a twig snake perhaps?

A *leguaan* scuttles across the path in search of a tasty morsel, Jamie notices the exquisite black and yellow patterns, recognizing it as a monitor. He jumps out of its way because he knows how painful a swipe from its tail can be. Xixi, energized by the coolness, swings from tree to tree, scaring roosting birds and causing a shower of leaves to fall in his path. He has found berries and is stuffing his face with them, purple rivulets dripping from his mouth. The sound of water is stronger now, the air misty. They are heading towards the waterfall and their favorite swimming pond.

Jamie cannot contain himself any longer, he runs, hops and skips towards the waterfall, strips off his clothes and jumps into the pool. Temba notices a piece of string hanging out of one of his pockets as they land on the ground and gazes kindly at the little mound in the pocket. She knows what it is and smiles. She takes her belt off and leaves it on a rock. Wrapping her skirt around her tightly she jumps in as well, squealing as she feels the rush of cold water against her skin.

The pool is deep and she imagines she has landed in a liquid world, silent and untroubled, she is at one with the water yet her insides quiver at what might lurk in the depths. As she surfaces, the loud crashing sound of the waterfall overpowers all other sounds and for a moment she forgets where she is. She just floats on her back, arms outstretched, eyes closed, enjoying the feeling of weightlessness. Her day dream is broken by something grabbing her legs and pulling her downwards. For a split-second she thinks 'crocodile' and then she punches out, feeling for the grip, a grip of soft, supple flesh belonging to Jamie. It is a game they play all the time, but today her thoughts were elsewhere and she had let her guard down. "Jamie, you bad, bad boy, one day I am going to die from fright"! she laughingly splashes him with water "you know how we must be careful of the Silent One."

"There are no crocodiles in this pond, only water snakes, and they are afraid of a big hippo like you!" he teases. Jamie disappears under water again and Temba treads water to the bank. As she climbs out, dripping wet, she feels distinctly uneasy, as if she were being watched. She peers into the shadows but sees nothing but the thick undergrowth. She hears the loud 'kwaa, kwaa, kwaa' sound of the *hadidah* birds. Those large, grey, long-beaked birds that are always around. She steps onto some green gung and hopping onto one foot, shrieks, "those hadidah birds! their droppings are huge!" Sitting on a warm rock streaked with gold veins, she tries to take the gluey pooh off the sole of her foot but it clings

so much that no amount of rubbing on the rock will budge it. She thinks, 'this does not come from a hadidah'. She looks straight at Jamie but in the corner of her eye catches a glimpse of something red flashing. She shivers, hugging herself. "Jamie get out of the water right now!" but Jamie is enjoying himself so much he does not hear her, or he pretends to not hear her.

Xixi, sitting at the edge of the pool, splashing in the shallows with his feet and little hands, freezes for a moment and then runs to Temba, shivering and twittering, clutching at her knees. Jamie ignores Temba and carries on diving under water and comes to the surface spewing water from his mouth in a spray, oblivious of the menace in the air.

"I'm a hippo, I'm a hippo, I can stay under the water for half a day if I like - I am so big I am afraid of nothing. I'm looking for tadpole shrimp but they are so tiny only someone with eyes like me can find them on the bottom of the pool." You are such a show off, thinks Temba, and so vulnerable. "Get out of the water, now," she says in a stern voice.

It is an idyllic scene, sun seeping through the heavy foliage, bird calls sounding like an orchestra, so why should Temba be shivering from fear and Xixi so upset? There is something unnatural in the air, evil and foul smelling. Jamie climbs out of the water, does a frenetic dance to shake off the droplets and heads for his clothes.

The moment is gone. All is back to normal. Pulling his pants on, he tugs at the string hanging from his pocket and out pops a furry little animal, whiskers twitching and little claws rubbing each other. "Hello Gerbi, you have been well behaved I hope? You haven't chewed my clothes, have you? Come, let me give you some water, you must be thirsty." Tenderly holding his pet, with a string tied around its middle he walks to the edge of the pond and scooping up water in his hand, offers it to the little animal.

"Mfana, I see you still have that rodent rat as a pet? Ugh, how can you love it?" Temba gives a dramatic shiver, "what use is he anyway? He sleeps all day."

"He is a *gerbil*, and he is the cleanest pet to have. He's a night animal, that is why he sleeps most of the day," replies Jamie quite sharply.

"Why does he have all that fur on his feet? asks Temba.

"As I have told you, he is a night animal, foraging for seeds and berries at night, but if he should move during the heat of the day, that hair on the soles of his feet protects him from the heat. He is no trouble at all and you must admit he is so cute. Xixi, give Gerbi some of those berries I saw you hiding in that tree trunk." Xixi scampers up the tree and brings back a handful for Gerbi and happily they eat the berries. Xixi has not always been this generous, it took a long time for Jamie to teach him to share. He would grab berries, nuts or stones and clutch them close to his body and refuse to share With patience Jamie played games of give and take with him, until Xixi realised it was okay to share. Xixi learnt that if he shared with others, others would share with him.

Even with humans, it is difficult to accept a new brother or sister and jealousy, 'the green-eyed monster,' stalks households for a while until with time and patience, the new sibling is accepted and everyone realizes that there is enough love and attention to go around in a family. Temba remembers how Zenze too had the odd tantrum and strange behavior when Jamie became the centre of attraction for the village and how now he would give his life for him. She takes Jamie by the hand and says "Mfana, Llanga (sun) of my day, come and sit here next to me, I have something important I need to tell you."

Tying the belt around her waist, under the shade of a cycad, one of the earth's oldest 'living fossils' with Xixi and Gerbi at their feet, Temba begins: "There are many

41

things that I want to tell you, that perhaps you will not understand. We, the people of Africa have many traditions that are passed on from one ancestor, the people who lived before us, to the other. Nothing is written, all our knowledge is passed from one storyteller to the other.

People lived in caves many, many years ago and sometimes, someone wanders into the depths of the caves and discovers tools, drawings and bits of bones that tell the story of long ago. These are sacred places because it is the resting place of our ancestors and they are tended and guarded with great care and respect. You came to us from the sky so how could you know of our customs? I have something very important to tell you, so please sit quietly and listen."

"No, No, I don't want to hear what you have to tell me. You look too serious and I can only imagine it is not good news. I would rather hear the story about how Zenze found me."

"I think Zenze should tell you your story, but how many times must we tell you?"

"I never get bored of hearing my story over and over again."

"Mfana, I have to tell you something that you should know. I am old enough to get married, and when the time comes, I have to leave you and the village and go and live elsewhere.

"No, you can't leave us, we are your family."

"Listen carefully, I have been promised in marriage to someone already, you know Drako. I don't love him, but I must obey the traditions of our people and I have to go anyway."

"I don't understand, I don't understand. Why can't you stay with us, why do you have to go away?"

"A wife has to follow her husband to his family, it's our custom."

"But I'll miss you," whispered Jamie as he turned around and pretended to look into the trees, wiping his tears and nose with his arm. "I knew I didn't want to hear your news," he said with a lump in his throat, as Gerbi scrabbled in the dirt at his bare feet and Xixi shuffled into the undergrowth to find something to eat.

Temba sighs and holds herself tightly, clutching her belt around her waist. How can she leave this special little boy?

"I think we should start making tracks towards home," said Temba with a tight throat, "the marogo will start wilting and not be fit for eating." She swallowed deeply and felt her words tremble as she spoke. Jamie made a loud sniffing sound and holding his nose exclaimed, "yuck!! there must be a dead animal close by - what a smell!" but gave a distinctly uneasy glance over his left shoulder and gingerly touched the little bundle of fur in his pocket. "Let's get out of this place and go and find some marula fruit for our father," said Jamie, "before elephants eat it all".

With Xixi on his shoulder, Gerbi in his pocket and pulling a stick behind him, Jamie followed Temba out of the clearing, occasionally looking behind him at the patterns the stick was making in the sand, but also to sneak a look just to be sure nothing or nobody was following them.

They paused in a clearing of multi-colored grasses, interspersed with purple and yellow flowers. A thousand and one red, orange and white butterflies with bright markings fluttered and dived between the small blossoms. Jamie kept slashing at the grasses with his stick, deep in thought.

CHAPTER 5

>>>><<<<<

.....no bird made that sound

Zenze squatted soundlessly behind the thorn bush, listening to his parents' conversation. This information was distressing, he vaguely knew about it, but from the anxiety in his parents' voices, he realized this was serious. He loved Temba and Jamie as if they were his blood brother and sister and did not want them to be unhappy. What was he to do? As his mother moved towards the *isigqolo* (container where corn is crushed), he snuck away and circled the kraal until he came to his 'thinking place' on the banks of the river. He collected a small mound of stones next to him and threw them into the water, trying to make them skim the surface a few times before they sank. This was a game he played with Jamie, who always beat him and he smiled thinking of how Jamie would throw up his arms, bend his knees, swivel his hips and scream "Yes!" when his stones skimmed the surface.

45

When was the right time to tell Jamie the entire story of his rescue? Should he tell him? Should he keep silent? He kept throwing stones while he thought of the day he found Jamie.

That fateful day, Zenze had been out since sunrise hunting for food and had gone to his favorite hunting area where he knew he would find hares. He had hunted a hare with his sling and tied it to his belt. The enormous outcrop of boulders was higher than all the forest around him and he loved the fact the he could see far into the distance. On the horizon he could see a thin spiral of smoke coming from the cooking fires of his kraal. Close to where he was standing, he knew, because he could hear it and had seen it many times, was the peaceful river winding through the valley. In places, though, it was noisy, thundering around boulders and down waterfalls, dangerous and forbidding. Shielding his eyes from the sun, he looked in the direction of a strange noise, a sputtering sound, a sound that did not belong in the forest. It was in the air – no bird made that sound. He caught a glint of something shiny.

Scrunching up his eyes, he followed the path of the sound until there was a loud noise, like thunder, crashing of broken branches, birds scattering into the air and then silence.

Zenze could make out some smoke rising from above the tree tops and decided to go and investigate. He could tell from the position of the sun that he should be making tracks back home, but his curiosity was too tweaked for him not to go and inspect. He clambered down the rocky outcrop, watching for tell tale signs, especially of *scorpions*, as this was a perfect environment for them. One sting from its tail could mean death. He saw a few rock rabbits scuttle away from him as he skirted the boulders heading towards the forest, their long ears flopping forwards and backwards, while their behinds bobbed up and down, spraying dust and small stones in their wake. Zenze felt his shoulders tense because he was going into a part of the forest he did not know well. He knew he was moving away from his kraal and a small tendril of fear crept into his stomach. What was he going to find? There was no path for him to follow so he wove around bushes and trees always moving crouched over in a hunter's stance towards the smoke.

He moved on and back into the forest which was now

in deep shadow. The ground underfoot was damp so the tracks were clear. He saw the spoor of a tortoise with its five claws on the forefoot and four on the hind feet.

He moved at a steady pace, keeping the sound of the river on his left side. He noticed many broken branches and tree trunks listing at an angle and immediately knew that elephant had walked this way. Of course, he knew that animals would be moving towards water at dusk, he only hoped that he wasn't going to meet up with any of the larger ones. At one point he was not sure of his bearings, so he climbed a stinkwood tree, causing a fluttering of wings as he disturbed some weaver birds. He saw the smoke still spiraling into the air but noticed something else.

On the ridge, next to the smoke, he saw a truck, the metal catching the last rays of the setting sun, one man on the back with binoculars and another one inside, looking at the smoke. These were strangers to the area and he had a bad feeling about them. He climbed down the tree and with a surge of energy, started sprinting towards the smoke.

A flock of quail loudly took flight from their scrubbing in the ground, scrounging for insects or seeds. He didn't even stop to look at them. He recognized their sound 'whic-which-ic', 'whic-whic-ic'. He kept his eyes on the ground and before long was within sight of the flames. Ahead of him loomed the enormous trunk of a baobab tree and he stealthily crept towards its shelter. He could hear murmurings that were human and felt anxious. He leopard crawled on his elbows until he could see clearly. He saw two mounds on the back of the truck, and caught a quick glimpse of what looked like golden hair before one of the men covered everything up with a blanket.

The two men were beating the flames with sticks and looking behind bushes near the plane. They were obviously looking for something, but Zenze could not hear what they were saying. Zenze, without understanding a word, had a feeling that these men were bad and their furtive looks told him that what they were doing was not an act of kindness but something wrong. He must have been holding his breath because he felt as if his lungs would burst. He did not move a muscle as he lay flat on his stomach, close to a huge root, becoming part of the approaching darkness. After a while, the men climbed into the truck and drove away. Zenze was sure they would come back in daylight to find what they were looking for.

As soon as the sound of the engine died away, Zenze, heart beating very fast, crept from behind the baobab tree and circled the smoldering wreckage. He had noticed tiny specks in the sky a little while ago and knew these were vultures circling. He suspected there was something dead or injured in the area, or perhaps they were circling for whatever was on that truck. While looking up in the sky, he didn't see a piece of hot metal on the ground and burnt the side of his foot. Muffling his scream he lay on the ground holding his leg. While on the ground he heard the distinctive call of the *hyena*, in fact it sounded like a laugh and the tendrils of fear crept up his spine. He knew that when hyenas laugh, they are hunting. Ignoring the pain in his foot, he skirted around the wreckage of the plane, then he heard the hyenas even closer and thought: 'the hare, they can smell the carcass that I have tied to my waist'.

He scanned the area from where he heard the hyena laughter and through some low bushes saw a pair of yellow eyes and the scuffling sound of many pads. He threw the dead hare towards the pack of hyenas, and watched as the hyenas lunged after it as a pack. Zenze picked up a piece of metal from the wreckage and started banging it with his spear and shouting as loud as he could. The hyenas slunk away heading for the dead hare, casting sly glances at Zenze. He pictured their very powerful jaws that could break up even elephant bones easily, and imagined their blunt, short claws tearing up the dead hare carcass. In their frenzy to tear the hare to shreds, they had turned from a bundle on the ground that was moaning and twitching. Zenze immediately knew it was a small child. Without thinking of his own safety, and ignoring the pain in his foot, he picked it up and ran for cover behind the Baobab tree. He had seen a big cavity in the trunk of the tree when he was hiding and gently placed the bundle inside. Next, he thought, I must make a fire to keep the hyenas and any other animal away and let my family know I need help.

He rushed around finding small dry sticks and looked towards the wreckage where he could see some smoldering embers. By blowing gently on them, he set a thin stick alight. From there it was easy to start a fire. By the light of the fire, he looked closely at the child – he thought it looked like a boy child but he was not sure. One of his legs was in a strange position, it was broken. The child also had a big gash on the head but it was still breathing. He knew he had to stop the leg from moving so he climbed a tree, cut two straight branches and used them as splints for the leg. He placed them on either side of the leg and wrapped them together with some tall grass. He looked around for the wild olive tree, he needed the leaves to cover the gaping wounds, all the while keeping alert to the sounds of the hyenas and any other animal around him. Luckily he had noticed a wild olive tree close by, and quickly plucked handfuls of the leaves. He heard the distant cough of a leopard and the roar of a lion, but felt they were far off and not dangerous, yet.

By this time it was virtually dark because night comes quickly in Africa and Zenze began to hear the noises of the night animals beginning to stir. The cicadas were chirping, an owl was hooting and nearby an *anteater* scraping with its long nose and claws at a termite mound for his daily feed of termites.

He needed water to wash the wounds and for the child to drink, but, his water gourd was empty. He limped to the river to collect some water. The fire would keep the hyenas away. He bent down on the river bank, dangling his gourd down when he saw a strange shape he thought was a rock. It was not a rock, but a small container, a box. It must have come from the aeroplane. He filled his gourd, grabbed the box and hobbled back to the tree. His mind was in chaos. So many things were happening all at once. He tucked the box right at the back of the tree cavity and focused his attention on the child. He poured water over the flapping skin on the child's leg and covered it with the leaves. Then he poured water on the head wound. Lifting his gourd to the child's lips he let the water drip slowly into its mouth.

He tried to make sense of what had just happened and wondered why those men had left a child and now thought.. the mounds on the back of the truck could have been the child's parents? If they knew there was a child, would they have left him? What were they looking for? The child? The box?. The child was groaning but warm, and the bleeding from the gash on his head had stopped.

He leaned his back against the enormous tree trunk convinced that he would be able to hear anyone or anything approaching him. He tended to his foot, wrapping wild olive leaves around it, tying it with long strands of fresh veld grass. He spoke out load saying, "surely my family will know by now that I'm in trouble and need help. I know they will follow the smoke from the fire." He listened intently for a while, but it had been a long, tension-filled day and he soon fell asleep.

Being a child of the wild, he did not respond to the normal sounds of the night. The cicadas 'creak, creaking' or the hippo's 'hrumph, hrumphing' way down on the riverside, foraging for food. Not even the 'snuff, snuffling' of the bushpig with its long snout and two smallish tusks, scrubbing for roots disturbed his sleep. Until all at once, he sat bolt upright, listening, fully awake. What had caused him to wake up? He listened intently, closing his eyes to hear better. Was it those two men? Had they noticed the fire and come back to investigate? It was definitely the sound of humans crashing through the foliage. He listened even more closely and made out the sound patterns of his father's speech. What a relief. He climbed out of the cavity in the baobab tree, waving his arms and shouted, "I'm here, I'm here." He made out human figures in the moonlight and then Temba, leading his old father was there before him, arms outstretched and he leaned into his embrace with a shudder of relief.

CHAPTER 6

....tula, tula tula, tula...

 ather, do not ask many questions, just believe what I tell you. In the cavity of that huge *baobab* tree lies a very injured little child with golden hair. I think two bad men have taken his mother and father away but were looking for something, either the child or something else. They will probably return at first light to search for whatever they were looking for, so we must take the boy away immediately and erase any signs that we were here." Zenze's father asked no more questions and gave out orders to the helpers who had followed him. They

55

immediately set to work to cover any signs that anyone had been there. Two took branches that were already broken and lying on the ground and swept all their tracks, walking backwards. Another two young boys did the same, going over what the first two had done, just to make sure.

Zenze had already earmarked a piece of straight metal from the wreck to be used as a stretcher and Kabo placed Jamie gently on it. Looking at Zenze's foot he said, "Nelson and I will carry the child, you take care of your foot and walk with us." First, the fire was doused and the ashes thrown into the river, while Kabo covered the area with fresh sand, strewn with some branches and old leaves. Kabo went around the area bent over almost double checking for any tell-tale signs they might have missed.

By looking at the footprints that were not theirs, Kabo and Zenza could tell that there had been two men, quite heavy men. They noticed some drag marks and surmised that something heavy had been dragged to the truck. Silently, making as little noise as possible they started their journey back to their kraal. Zenze had felt the gentle touch of Temba on his shoulder while he was about to pick up Jamie, and she spoke silently and said, "Kabo and

Nelson will carry the child, you walk with me and father." He knew she had come to see that he was safe and to be Shaka's eyes. As he limped away from the wreckage, he noticed Temba making extra sure that no clues were left – she had good eyes, in fact she was known as 'eagle eyes'. The hyenas were still fighting each other for the last morsel of the rabbit carcass and pairs of yellow eyes followed their every move, too cowardly to come forward but hoping for something to scavenge later on.

They walked through the night with only the moonlight to guide them. Shaka had given the order that there was to be no talking and everyone walked with their own thoughts. They passed a rhino midden, of that everyone was certain because the stench was very bad. Catching Zenze's eye, Temba pinched her nose and scrunched up her face, to which he smiled and nodded. Strange, thought Temba, that rhinos always used the same spot for their toileting. She was glad that rhinos usually slept at night, she really didn't want to meet one tonight. On they walked, the forerunners making a path for the stretcher-bearers. Zenze had started to limp a little but said nothing to anybody. One of the boys had run ahead to alert Refilwe to prepare for an injured child.

At one point they needed to cross the river, the

boys knew of a place where it was narrow with stepping stones, so they headed towards it. At the stepping stones, where a thick mist made them look eerie and floaty, they made a human chain and helped everyone across, especially Kabo and Nelson who were trying to keep the limp body of Jamie from falling into the water. Zenze guided Shaka holding his hand, and with the help of Temba and the village helpers, they made their way across the river.

The river was fast flowing so the threat of crocodiles was not great, but they all knew that one false step and it could signal danger. Again, one of the boys went back into the forest and erased their footprints and any signs of their passing. Zenze was now in territory that he knew, and pointed in the direction he wanted to take.

He knew they had left the forest and were in the open grasslands, scattered with trees and bushes. Because these bushes and grasses provided abundant food for many browsing and grazing animals, he was alert as it was 'lion country'. A few weeks ago, he had seen a pride of lion in the area, with many cubs, making the lionesses more protective and aggressive.

The child moaned and groaned in his sleep, every bump caused him pain. The smell of wood fires alerted everyone they were near home and a solitary drum beat welcomed them back. Shaka trailed behind, using a stick to help him walk and leaning on Zenze. His thoughts were troubled, nothing like this had ever happened before. He needed to talk to Zenze alone, to get all the details. He would throw the bones tonight and pray to his ancestors for guidance. He stopped dead in his tracks and gripped Zenze's wrist. He had the feeling that they were being watched. It could not have been the bad men as they would have heard them. He was disoriented and could not pinpoint what direction his uneasiness was coming from.

Temba too was transfixed. Rubbing her arms, she tried to flatten the goose bumps that had appeared, yet it was a warm night. They were crossing a patch of soggy grass and mud but to Temba's disbelief, she saw the mud bubbling and giving off a thin mist of putrid smell. Her stomach rolled over and bile climbed to her throat. Before she could say anything Shaka trembled and mumbled to no one in particular. "Something evil is at large tonight."

Refilwe, alerted to their homecoming had stoked up the fire opposite their hut, and was anxiously waiting for them. She was looking in particular for Zenze and at the sight of him limping ran towards him with outstretched arms. "My son, my son, what happened to you?" I am so happy to see you. Come and sit down."

"I am fine, it is just a small cut. Please tend to the child, he is badly wounded." Only then did Temba turn her attention to the child on the makeshift stretcher and immediately bend down to look at him. She raised her hands to cover her mouth to stifle a gasp, she was so shocked. "Who is this child? Where has he come from? Why is he wounded? Why is he alone?" she asked looking around at Zenze, Temba and Nelson. "Answers later, I must help him now."

Shaka felt his way into the hut. He touched Refilwe on the top of her head. He lay down on his blanket on the floor and fell into a deep sleep with the sound of Refilwe singing a soft lullabye to the unconscious child.

Tula tu, tula tula tula baba

Sleep my little one the wind is blowing

Tula tu, tula tula tula baba

The bright star is shining just for you

Tula tula tula baba, hush my baby don't you cry

CHAPTER 7

....when you touch each bead...

emba walked into the hut to help Refilwe with the boy. She had never seen a boy with such light coloured skin and straight white hair before and felt anxious that he might be a ghost and said so to Refilwe. "He is not a ghost, my child, just a little boy whose skin is pale. He has the same blood in his veins as you do and I'm sure behaves just like all the other little boys in the kraal. Help me wash him and see whether we can give him some water. Zenze is right – his leg is broken and the wound to his head does not look too bad, but it needs to be cleaned. Zenze did such a good job. I have soaked some more wild olive leaves to help close his wounds so that they do not become infected and then when he wakes up we'll decide what to do."

Temba gasped and thought she would faint when she saw a bone sticking out of his trouser legs. At that moment, the boy moaned. "Mommydaddy, mommydaddy." "He must be calling out for his parents – it must be, I would," said Temba. "Poor little boy, I wonder where he comes from and what his story will be. I will give him the name 'Mfana' little boy."

Refilwe gently cut the trouser legs with a knife. "At least it is a clean break, we'll have to put the two ends of the bone back together". Again the boy moaned "mommydaddy, sore sore." Refilwe gently poured a dark liquid against his lips and trickled it down his throat. "This will make him sleep so that he does not feel any pain for a while". With sure movements she washed the leg and the wound with warm, boiled water, put the two pieces of bone together, covered the wound with the leaves, then took strips of clean cloth and bandaged the leg. She again tied the two branches to his leg and made it all quite tight so that the leg would not move. Temba noticed that Refilwe looked very tired and wiped the sweat off her brow with slow movements. How she loves this lady who looked after her as if she were her mother. "It has been a long night, sweet mother, you go and sleep a little, I will watch over him."

"If he stirs, give him water and just dab a little of this liquid on his lips. Thank you, I am really very tired."

She curled on the floor next to Shaka and fell asleep immediately.

By the light of the moon, with odd bits of scraggly cloud crossing its face, filtering through the front opening and the dying embers of the fire Temba watched the sleeping child. So many questions went through her mind. Who was he? Who was with him when he fell out of the sky? Where was he going? Who were those men who took something away with the truck? Would someone come to fetch him? Would he die? She wiped his brow with a damp cloth, and moved the silky hair away from his eyes, feeling such tenderness that she had never felt before. She could imagine just how confused and sad he would be when he finally awoke completely, because she too had been left on her own as a toddler and had cried many nights for her mother.

While looking at Mfana she dozed off and dreamt..........

"Temba, go and wash your hands and come and help me knead the bread dough," said Ntsepe, her mom. Temba remembers her mom's voice, always laughing and singing, never a harsh word. "I know you prefer running around like a squirrel, getting up to mischief with your cousin Zenze, but you are a girl and have to learn certain tasks, and one of them is how to bake bread." Temba smiles in her dream as she remembers.

"Oh! Do I really have to?" Temba hears her whiney voice and sees herself scrunching her nose and twisting her mouth. She remembers that she always did this to her mom because she liked to see her make "slit, snake-eyes" at her, while her lips curved ever so little at the ends in a hidden smile. She now admits that as a child, like all children, she loved getting attention from her mom, even if it meant 'putting on a show'! She would often do silly things like drop a gourd so her mom would look at her, or behave in a way that she knew she was not supposed to, like stand on something wobbly, put things in her mouth, or pretend to not hear, just to be the centre of her mom's attention. She remembers how she was jealous when Ntsepe spoke to anyone but her and how she would grab her by her skirt and drag her away to show her something or need something urgently, especially if it was another child. Oh! hundreds of things! She could still hear herself wailing "mama I want you, I need you".

Temba woke up and looked at the child, but the dream had made her remember her childhood.

Temba actually loved kneading the bread dough with her mom, in fact, she liked doing anything that meant she could be alone with her mother. She loved her smell, the way she made her feel special when she caught sight of her, calling her 'mtwana', "my princess." She remembers the way her mom braided her hair with small multicolored beads, how she loved to snuggle into her neck and giggle while her mom tickled her saying "here come my ant friends" – she never tired of that game. She remembers how she was already quite a big child and begged Ntsepe to strap her to her back as she did when she was a baby. Refilwe had to help hoist Temba onto Ntsepe's back amidst much laughing and teasing. Ntsepe danced the dance of the maidens in the red dust at the centre of the kraal with a rather heavy Temba on her back. How happy and secure Temba felt against her mom's warm back, she really felt so special. Whenever she touches her bead necklace, it reminds her of her mom, who always wore lots of beads, around her neck and waist. Every color had a meaning and a message.

While Ntsepe strung beads she had said to Temba, "you will always be able to remember me when you touch each bead. This yellow one is for sunshine, that all your days may be happy and full of our beautiful, hot African sun. White beads are for peace, not only in our country but within yourself. That you may find peace in your life and how you live your life. Don't be greedy and envious, be generous. This green one is so that you will always have food on your table for your family. Learn how to grow food, tend the plants and you will be rewarded. This blue bead is that you may never be thirsty and that you look after and not pollute the waters of our land. Water is life and without it, life cannot exist. Do not waste it. Whenever you see a flowing river, give thanks. One day I wish that you will see the big oceans of the world. You might wonder why we have to look after our rivers when there is so much water in the ocean, but remember that sea-water is salty and cannot be drunk or used to water the fields. This purple bead is for honesty. I wish you to be honest with yourself and towards others. Don't look for the blame in others but take responsibility for your actions. And this red one, my princess, the most important of all is for love. My love for you has no beginning and no end and no matter what you do, where you go, how you do what you do, I will always love you. Little did Temba know that she would have to remember the words that accompanied the beads so often and so soon.

The child stirred. She lifted his head and squeezed some water onto his lips. Feeling content from her dream, she had a flash back to a time when she was ill and Ntsepe had stayed by her side until she was better. No matter when she woke up, she was there, giving her water, holding her hand and murmuring sweet nothings to her until she fell asleep again.

Temba thought about her dream and longed to be that child again, to be loved and nurtured and to feel protected and safe. She knew that the day when she would be given away in marriage was coming closer and closer. She had heard whisperings that she was to be given to Drako as his wife – a thought that terrified her. She did not like him. When they played together as little children he would always try to push her against trees and hold her so tight she would scream to get loose. In the deepest part of her, she knew that her childhood friend Ami was the one she wanted to marry, but in her culture she could not oppose the will of her parents. If they had chosen Drako as her husband, she would have to marry him, no questions asked.

Thinking about it, Shaka and Refilwe were not really her parents, they were her aunt and uncle. Ntsepe was Refilwe's sister. Ntsepe was her real mother, but how could she find her to ask her to oppose her marriage to Drako? Ntsepe herself had been unwillingly given away in marriage to Wakiri's son and had not been able to take Temba with her. Temba was left in the care of her family and raised by Refilwe as her own child. Wakiri was a powerful chief of chiefs and his word and orders were never questioned. He had seen Ntsepe dancing at the festival of the maidens and was immediately smitten by her beauty and grace. Her light olive skin and almond shaped eyes bewitched him and he could think of no one else for his son. Unknown to anyone, Ntsepe and Petri, childhood friends, had promised to marry one day. However, while working in the city to make enough money to build a house for them, Petri, Temba's father, had been killed, leaving Ntsepe alone to look after Temba. He had never seen his daughter, Temba.

Refilwe and Shaka accepted this little girl as if she was their granddaughter with great joy, they spoilt her as grandparents do, she could do no wrong. "She is the most beautiful and special child in the whole world," they told everyone. "She may not have a father but she has her mother, us and a home where she will be loved and nurtured."

Temba was so deep in her thoughts that she did not hear the soft shuffling footfalls and nearly jumped 'out of her skin' when a hand touched her on her shoulder. It was Zenze with a gourd of warm goat's milk and porridge.

"Little sister, you need to eat and drink a little. Sleep a while, I'll watch the little boy, then I'll wake you up just before sunrise as I need to do something." Immediately she looked keenly at him and whispered, "what are you going to do"?

"You don't need to know all my movements – miss-nose-in-everyone's business, I'll tell you when you wake up."

"No! you'll tell me now else I won't go to sleep."

"You are such a *tick*, once you latch on you don't let go. Okay, I'll tell you but you are not to tell anyone else. Shaka my father knows, but no one else. If my mother knew she would worry her insides into a knot. I have a feeling that those bad men will go back to the place where we found the child. I think they were looking for something, maybe the child and maybe not. I want to go back and look around in the light of day." He purposefully did not tell her about the box he had hidden, he thought to keep it a secret for a while longer.

"Please be very careful, I could not stand it if something bad happened to you," said Temba, and she squeezed his hand. Zenze moved his hand away roughly.

"Don't get all soppy on me – I'll be fine, nothing is going to happen to me. The warm milk and her extreme tiredness got the better of her and she did not even answer him, she crawled under a blanket and fell fast asleep.

CHAPTER 8

....look for a box...

enze felt bad that he had not told Temba all the details, but was so unsure himself that he thought it better to keep some thoughts to himself. He was concerned for her. He recalled the conversation he'd overheard between his mother and father about Temba being promised to Drako in marriage. Ugh! he detested that pompous, selfish, bully of a boy. Whenever Drako's father visited Shaka, the boys were thrown into each other's company and would wander down to the river to throw stones or look for frogs, like boys usually do. As soon as they were out of sight of the adults, Drako would begin his bullying, physical and verbal. He would wait for Zenze to be on a rock and then push him into the water, laughing, no, evilly guffawing, and mocking him saying "you are a little squirt, I could drown you if I wanted to, you are nothing but the lowly son of a lesser chief, whereas I am a great chief's

71

nephew. You will never be anything in your life, whereas one day I could be chief. You are a coward, I dare you to tattle tale on me like a girl, girlie, girlie, girl." Whenever he could he tripped Zenze or punched him on the same spot on his upper arm knowing it would eventually bruise. He harassed him at every turn he could, just like bullies do.

Zenze seethed inside and did not retaliate because he knew his father would be held responsible for Zenze's actions and it would always come down to Drako's word against his, and he knew Drako would be believed. "There are always bullies in the world," Shaka had once told him, "they are cowards and losers with no respect for themselves or others. The only way they know to feel good about themselves is to belittle someone else. It takes a great man or woman to stand up to bullies and show indifference. Once you show you don't care, and do not take the bait, they will lose interest." Zenze held onto these words, feeling the bile rising in his throat when Drako put his arm around Zenze and called him "my friend" in his father's presence. "One day, one day", Zenze used to think, "one day I will get my chance to show you who the coward is".

He heard a gritting sound and realized he was grinding his teeth. He was so anxious that just the thought of Drako made him tense all over. How could he let his beloved Temba marry that person who was worse than a hyena dropping, stinkier than a rhino's midden and slimier than a crocodile's lair! Like leopards, he knew that bullies do not change their spots and Drako would bully Temba, once she was his wife. Ooh!, how he hated bullies.

Just before the sun peeked over the horizon, when the world is silent, as if it were waiting for a painter to add sunlight and nature begins to awaken, Zenze shook Temba's shoulder and whispered, "I'm leaving now, see you soon." Leaving the hut in such a hurry that later, all she could remember was a blur and Zenze saying "see you soon." She covered herself with a blanket, hugging it to her and facing the little boy, continued her vigil. Zenze must have added wood to the fire as she could hear it crackling.

Zenze had a little bundle tied around his waist with some *biltong* (dried meat) and a gourd for water. He was very capable of surviving in the bush, knew what berries to eat, where to look for roots and also where to dig for water, and today he needed to have something to sustain him while he kept watch on the wreckage of the plane. At a slow pace, his foot was still a little tender, he jogged away from the kraal, the air thick with wood smoke and the smell of smoldering fires. The grey dog opened one eye, saw it was Zenze, wagged its tail and carried on sleeping. He ran down the small hill at the back of the kraal and almost immediately entered an area of thick bush.

His bare feet, calloused from continual use, did not feel the jagged stones he trampled. He jogged on silently alert. Rounding a corner he stopped in his tracks to let a slow moving *porcupine* waddle away. He stood dead still, knowing that if the porcupine felt threatened he would probably present its rear end, raise its quills, stamp its feet, grunt ferociously while rattling its hollow tail quills. The quills are not poisonous but if a quill embeds itself into a predator's body it could cause death through infection. The porcupine being a nocturnal animal, Zenze thought it was probably going back to its burrow with a full tummy. He continued jogging, aware his surroundings were becoming brighter – he loved the dawn, that particular time between night and day when for an instant the world seems to stop in its tracks and an invisible hand washes all rough edges leaving a spotless, smooth earth.

On he ran, stopping at a little stream to fill his water gourd and take a few mouthfuls of water from his hand. He took note of the direction he needed to travel and no longer ran but walked quickly with his shoulders hunched forward, crouched closer the ground. He was looking for new markings, he could not see the tracks they had left the night before, but some, like the broken branch on his right he had made on purpose to help him today. He knew he was on the right track when he smelt the rhino midden.

Early morning sunlight filtered through some Acacia trees and Zenze squinted up his eyes, he had seen a slight movement. Yes, as he suspected it was a herd of *Nyala* buck. He could see the white chevron between the eyes and white stripes down their sides with some white spots on their lower haunches. He picked out the leading bull with its shaggy coat, large horns and predominant ivory tip. He took in the rust colored coat and the giveaway "orange socks" of the Nyala cows and carried on moving towards his destination.

He needed to cross a patch of grasslands where he would be exposed to lion, so he moved towards a large outcrop of stones making use of their shadow. He skirted around the rocks; he was nearing his destination, he could smell the burnt veld-grass. Quietly, watching his path carefully for fear of making even the slightest sound, he moved towards a spot a little higher than the plane wreck and lay down to wait in the shade of a *kokerboom* (quiver tree). He chewed on a piece of biltong and watched a spider weave its web, dripping with early morning dew.

He gave a huge, silent yawn. He hadn't slept much last night and had travelled quite far this morning. His eyelids felt heavy and, leaning his back against the trunk of the tree, gripping his knees, he lay his head on them and was immediately asleep. It wasn't the sound of a little field mouse scampering from under a rock, or the rushing of the river over the rocks, not even the distant sound of a wild pig scavenging for roots that woke him up, but the "goway, goway" sound of two loerie birds in the branches directly above him. He woke up with a start and lay perfectly still. What was that sound? It was a sound not often heard in these parts, it was a motor engine. He had been right. The bad men were coming back. He heard the sound of the engine stop and four people stepped out of the truck, two white and two brown men. He recognized one of the brown men – his name was Sneakiti. He had been banished from Shaka's kraal for stealing and selling goats that did not belong to him. The four spoke a mixture of Juju and a foreign language. Zenze understood the Juju.

The four men took sticks and began rummaging in the debris. Zenze heard Sneakiti say to his friend, "look for a box, that is what they want us to find." Haauw! thought Zenze, they are not looking for the boy, they are looking for the box. The white men were obviously not trained in tracking as they did not even bother to see whether others had been there, but Sneakiti was wise to the bush and its tracks and at times looked a little puzzled at what he saw. They stopped for a drink of water from a gourd and then continued poking with sticks and heaving pieces of metal around, looking underneath. At one stage, Sneakiti, searching around in thick vegetation screamed and started cleaning his trouser pants legs. He had startled a striped weasel that had squirted a foul, oily liquid at him, thinking him an enemy. It would be days before the smell vanished. Zenze tried his best to stifle a roar of laughter, 'serves him right,' he thought.

"Don't stop looking, I don't pay you to stand around doing nothing" shouted one of the white men. What a horrible sounding tone of voice, thought Zenze, he was very sure now that these were not good men. Zenze's heart stopped when after a while they headed towards the baobab tree, looking for a cool place to rest and have something to eat. Zenze was so afraid they would find him, that he started sweating. Sneakiti stopped and said, "I do not want to sit under a big tree, I am afraid of the tampan ticks that like to live under large trees." With a resigned air the four of them stopped under a smaller thorn tree and ate some food, it looked like bread and meat. Whew! Zenze could not believe his luck.

Zenze was so close he could smell the food and his tummy began to rumble. The two men told Sneakiti and his friend to carry on looking for the box, while they rested. Within a few moments they were lying, sprawled in the shade and snoring, while Sneakiti and friend probed listlessly here and there all the while talking, much to Zenze's delight.

"I wonder what is so important about that box that he would pay us to find it," said Sneakiti. "Maybe it has gold or diamonds in It — the white man is always looking for those things." He had a brainwave and said. "Listen, my friend, if we find the box we won't tell them, then we'll come back and see what is inside. If it is gold or diamonds, we'll keep it for ourselves, if not, we'll sell it to them at a later stage, we'll say someone else found it and we bought it from them."

"You are so clever," said his friend, "why did I not think of that?" With that thought in mind they attacked the bush around the wreckage with vigor, flinging all sorts of objects into the air. Zenze's keen eyes missed nothing. While they were lifting pieces of the plane, they were so set on looking for a box, they displaced a small red object but did not notice it. All that was visible of the object was a tiny metal tip. Zenze marked the place in his mind and waited, and waited.

He was hungry and thirsty but did not move a muscle. A playful troupe of monkeys swung from tree to tree watching the men. A little *meerkat* came out of its burrow a few feet away from where Zenze lay. Its light fawn colored body a perfect camouflage for the surroundings. It sat on its hind legs, little arms held in front watching the goings on with curiosity. Zenze noticed the conspicuous black rings around its eyes and the slender black tipped tail that tapered to a point. The meerkat watched a while, whisked its tail from side to side and disappeared down into the cool of its burrow. After what seemed like hours, the men woke up, stretched, scratched, saw that no box had been found , made signs to Sneakitii and friend to get back into the truck and drove away in a cloud of dust. The two Loeries in the tree chased each other calling, "goway, goway."

The first thing Zenze did was stretch his numb legs, drink some water and chew on some biltong. He was certain that he could not leave the box in the baobab tree but had to hide it somewhere else. But where? Those two, Sneakiti and friend, would be back tomorrow for certain and possibly find it.

All at once, he knew exactly where he was going to hide it, but it was getting late and he had to hurry. He stepped into the cavity of the tree, took hold of the box and carrying it in the crook of his arm, started in the direction a little out of the way of his kraal, but first he bent down and picked up a little red toy. He headed towards a hill, with rocks strewn all over it as if a giant had placed these boulders as protection. This was a sacred place where ancestors were buried. Here and there aloes grew, their thorny, thick, fleshy leaves a danger to eyes and arms. At this moment he noticed they were in flower, beautiful, tall, red flowers that looked like red hot pokers. A bee-eater perched on a flower, grasshopper in its mouth that it had just caught, glared at Zenze as if he were a trespasser. As he climbed he felt the heat radiating from the boulders that had been baking in the sun the whole day. He knew he would see hyraxes (they look like huge rats) here because they loved to bask in the sun absorbing the heat.

Zenze climbed until he was almost at the summit and then stopped at a boulder. He pushed a bush aside very carefully so as to not break any branches, hoping that none of the bees buzzing around the small flowers would sting him. He lay on his tummy and pushing the box ahead of him, slid into a hole concealed by the bush. It was so dark he could not see his hand but he had been here before so he knew there would be some light soon. He crawled on his stomach for a few seconds and then started seeing pale light. When he reached the end of the tunnel, light filtered in from somewhere above him and the sound of running water was close.

He could now stand up. He caught his breath, as people always do when struck with awe. He was in an enormous cave with a stream running through it. Next time, he would come prepared with fire torches so he could see more of the cave. There were tunnels that had never been explored and a darkness in corners that was frightening. He felt for the cave wall and counted ten steps to the right and put the box down, with the little red tractor on top. He turned around, counted ten steps and found the opening to the tunnel, crawled out, patted the bush into place again and headed for home, picking up his food pouch from where he had hidden it.

His stomach was rumbling so loudly he felt all the animals could hear him. He smiled, everything had gone well. The baddies had not found the box and as far as he could tell they were not looking for the boy. He crossed the stream and halfway through bent down to wash his face vigorously, took a mouthful of water, swished it around his mouth and spat it out. Ah! he felt better. While he was at it, he jumped right in, bent down until he was under water, blew bubbles, surfaced, shook himself, climbed out and headed towards the path. Soon he was close enough to the kraal to smell the fires and hear the dogs barking. He went straight to Shaka's hut, scattering some chickens pecking for worms and insects near the entrance. Refilwe looked up, smiled and said. "Where have you been Zenze, or better still, don't tell me, I'm just happy that you are back. The boy is alive but has many injuries. I am giving him my special muti (medicine) that will keep him sleeping for a long while, so that his bones can heal. Be a good son and bring me some warm goat's milk for breakfast. I can think of food, now that you are back." Zenze bowed to his mother, with his hand over his heart and went outside.

CHAPTER 9

....they made believe she did not exist...

"P ound, pound, pound," beat the wooden mallet against the sides of the *isigqolo* container holding the corn. Refilwe pounded the corn without much thought to what she was doing, her thoughts were far away. The kraal was quiet, except for some infants chasing a chicken nearby, the shrieking and laughing of the children mixing with the squawking of the chickens. Her spirit was troubled and she needed to be doing something repetitive to ease the heaviness she felt, thinking of Temba's future.

Refilwe's marriage to Shaka had also been arranged by their parents who knew each other well. Shaka had been a playmate of hers, so she had just naturally moved from being a friend to a wife and then subsequently a mother. She knew that loving someone meant being kind to each other. She had had only one child, Zenze whom she adored, however, fate had given her a niece Temba, and then Mfana to look after. She had brought up all three children as if they were her own. It made no difference to her that two were adopted. She loved, nurtured, scolded and disciplined them evenly. Now that they were growing up, the decisions concerning them that had to be made, were more difficult and more complex, and she was finding it difficult to 'let go'. She would have loved to have kept them all close to her and not have them far away, but she knew that life was not like that. Children grew up and made their own lives and travelled their own paths, a mother could only do what she did best, love them no matter what, and when the time was right, let them go. Her thoughts floated to her sister Ntsepe. When she was a young girl, Wakiri noticed her grace and beauty and decided he wanted her for his son. He did not consider whether she would want to be his bride, whether she liked him or whether they had anything in common. He sent Horrifendi, his witchdoctor to Shaka's kraal, to organize the marriage. He ordered Refilwe to ready Ntsepe for the time when she would become Wakiri's son's bride. A bride price or lobola was set. 50 cows, 50 goats, 20 sheep as well as 10 blankets for the elders, two new three-legged pots, and

5 spears were agreed on. Ntsepe had no part in any of the dealings, it was all done by Horrifendi and Shaka.

On a specified day, according to tradition ten bare backed horsemen came to the village, herding the cows, goats and sheep, and Refilwe could not restrain her tears. She knew they had come to take Ntsepe away. As was the custom, the bridal party, consisting of Horrifendi and nine of his guides spent the night under a tree in the meeting place called an *isigcawua*. A feast had been prepared for the next day and the entire village invited. An ox and six goats were slaughtered and the women had been cooking vegetables and brewing beer for days.

Before that special day, Ntsepe had spoken for many hours with her sister Refilwe about Temba, her future and her dreams. Ntsepe had made shawls, beaded necklaces and a special belt for her infant daughter with as much love as she could with a heavy heart. She knew she would not see her grow up into a beautiful woman, and made Refilwe promise that she would keep her memory alive and to try at all costs to let them be reunited one day. Because Temba was not a child born in Wakiri's kraal, he had not allowed her to accompany Ntsepe.

In preparation for her marriage, Ntsepe was given special treatment by the women. She was bathed, rubbed with scented oils and her every need seen to. Her hair was oiled and braided with beads and her arms and ankles bedecked with beaded ornaments. What everyone noticed, though, was the look of sorrow in her eyes. All she wanted to do was hug her child, Temba, and talk to her sister. She held her child's face and traced the outlines of her mouth, eyes, ears, cheeks and nose as if she could imprint them in her mind forever. She whispered, "don't forget me, don't forget me" into her tiny, perfect ears.

Marriage celebrations were festive affairs and spanned over a few days giving both sides of the families time to get to know each other, but Wakiri's kraal was too far and its location a closely guarded secret, so only the guests that had come to fetch Ntsepe were present. The bridegroom remained at his kraal awaiting her arrival. There would be another celebration when she arrived at her new home. Ntsepe knew that she would be blindfolded near to the entrance of Wakiri's kraal as it was kept a close secret. No one knew the way into the kraal. – How was she ever going to see her sister and child again?

Ntsepe's bridal clothes were made of a thick cloth with bright red, blue and white beads worked into the detail. Her headdress too was encrusted with beads of all colours, lovingly sewn into the material by the young maidens of the village. While the wedding guests ate and danced to drum beats, Ntsepe sat in her wedding clothes, her face covered by a veil, under the shade of a tree, surrounded by the young girls of the tribe and her beloved sister. Such urgent last minute requests and promises were made between the two sisters. "I don't want to go, please don't make me! Please remember to ...., don't forget to....... don't let her forget me, don't forget me, don't forget me." Of course Temba had been sent to visit a nearby aunt to keep her out of sight. Wakiri's people did not want to acknowledge her. They made believe she did not exist.

During the wedding festivities, while maidens moved in a rhythmic dance, causing the dusty earth to coat their feet in a red film, singing and clapping hands, Horrifendi, sat on a rock covered in animal skins next to Shaka. Whereas Shaka listened happily to the partying, Horrifendi's look was so severe that Refilwe shuddered. He had a look of foreboding and evil around him. She found him disgusting. My poor, poor Ntsepe – I fear for your future, she thought as she cried.

Finally, at daybreak it was time for Ntsepe to leave her home for the last time. During the night, in secret,

Refilwe had brought Temba to her. Everything that had had to be said between the sisters had been said, so she just rocked her child to sleep and kept her in her arms all night. She hugged her little girl and put a string of beads around her neck saying, "remember me when you touch these beads and when you see the sun rise in the morning and the stars sparkle at night because I will be thinking of you at that precise moment as well. I will never forget you."

Ntsepe left her kraal on horseback, her eyes closed, not looking back – the pain was too much to bear.

When Temba was growing up and needed reassurance, Refilwe hugged the toddler to her and spoke to her of her mother. She kept her promise to her sister and always pointed to the stars and said, "your mama is thinking of you at this very moment and her eyes are sparkling like those shining stars, there is not a moment in the day or night that she is not thinking of you. Touch the bead necklace around your neck and she will be thinking of you.

Now, many years later, Temba is at an age when girls were ready for marriage. She, however, wanted to marry Ami her childhood companion and again Wakiri had intruded in their lives and had called for her to be his Nephew's wife, the ugly bully, Drako. 'Oh! if only Ntsepe could intervene', thought Refilwe. Maybe, maybe now was the time for a journey to the secret kraal. It was dangerous and long, but with Jamie and Zenze as companions, it could be done.

And now she had the problem of Jamie as well. They had not told him that maybe one or both of his parents were alive because they were protecting him from those bad men. It had taken a long time for Jamie to recover from his wounds and the time had never seemed right and the language barrier too great to explain everything to him. He had lost most of his memory at the time of his accident and was only lately beginning to remember some of his language. His parents were coming to him in dreams. He'd say, "the lady with the golden hair came to me in my dreams." Sometimes, "a big, happy man with hair on his face carried me on his shoulders."

Shaka had sworn his entire kraal to secrecy about Jamie and no one outside the kraal even knew that he existed. News from the outside world had filtered through from one of the men who had made a trip to the closest town. The gossip was that Jamie's parents were both missing in the forest, his father a famous chemist and his mother a doctor, but both had probably been eaten by wild animals as no trace had been found. There had not been a mention of a son.

Refilwe remembers how she had kept Jamie sedated for a long time while his bones and injuries healed, and how slowly, slowly he regained consciousness. She remembers that look of terror and insecurity when he saw their strange faces and home. He could not express himself but she understood him and would hold his hand or hug him closely. A child loves and needs to be hugged, there is no more potent medicine. He took an immediate liking to Temba and Zenze and they to him. Temba dressed his wounds and made funny faces for him, so that he could learn to laugh again, while Zenze brought him berries from the forest as a treat. He would laugh out loud when Temba pretended her finger was a worm, tickling his arm as her finger crept toward his armpit singing, "there's a worm at the bottom of the forest and his name is wiggly wooo." Zenze would also bring poisonous berries and mushrooms and shake his head, "no, no, no," make spitting noises, hold his tummy, roll on the ground and make dreadful faces and noise to show him that they were poisonous.

One day, Zenze brought Jamie a baby gerbil and it was exactly what he needed. Jamie tended the little rat with such tenderness and love, it made Refilwe shake her head in wonder. Jamie was so afraid of losing Gerbi, that's what he called him, that he attached a little cord around its body, but of course Gerbi chewed his way through it in no time. However, Jamie kept on tying the cord around Gerbi until he was so used to it he no longer chewed it. Zenze taught Jamie what seeds to feed Gerbi and from that first day they were inseparable. Gerbi lived in Jamie's pocket, and the only evidence that he was there was the bit of cord hanging out of his pocket. Jamie learnt to walk again with Zenze and Temba propping him up on either side, every day he learnt new words so that soon he could communicate his needs.

Refilwe pounded the corn so fine, she had to smile. Her thoughts had been so far away and so intense that her arms had moved of their own will. She thought that if Ntsepe could hear her daughter's problem, she could talk to Wakiri and not marry her off to Drako. Ntsepe had made the supreme sacrifice of leaving her daughter and marrying into Wakiri's kraal, surely he would be kind and see her reasoning. Refilwe's great fear was Horrifendi, the witchdoctor. He had no kindness and cared for no one. Horrifendi, was Chief Wakiri's right hand man and because they had grown up together there was a loyalty bond between them.

Horrifendi had a following of people loyal to him only through fear and threats. No one dared say anything against him or not obey his every wish. People were known to disappear if they did not obey him. He was known to brew revolting and smelly concoctions in the middle of the night. Animals stopped their calls and became silent when he was around. A friend of Zenze had told him that Horrifendi did not have red blood in his veins but yellow slime and that he had a tail under his loin cloth. His breath was so foul that leaves wilted when he breathed on them and that with only a look he could kill a man. Zenze did not believe this, but a trickle of fear spread down his back.

And Jamie, what was in store for him? If his parents were alive, would they not have come looking for him? Who were those bad men Zenze had seen when he found Jamie? Why had no one come to look for Jamie? Once, some young boys out hunting had come across an old man, so close to death he had only just survived the trip back to the village, but had continually repeated 'maaisan'. Shaka and Refilwe had not understood the message he was trying to tell them.

Refilwe heard the sound of feet behind her, and

without turning knew it was Shaka, using his stick to find her and shuffling his feet. Even though he was now completely blind, he could find his way around the kraal, as long as no one changed the position of objects.

"I can sense that you are very troubled," he said, "I could hear you pounding the corn with such force and only came by to save the *'isigqolo'* bowl" his lips turned up at the corners in a smile. He lay his hand on her shoulder murmuring, "you are right, we need to talk to our children about their future. I need to cleanse my spirit before I talk to them. I need to be sure that I lead them in the right direction.

CHAPTER 10

...we need to prepare...

haka sat crossed legged in front of a fire in the middle of a clearing in the deep forest. He rubbed his knees trying to ease the pain that ate at his bones. "It's old age," he would say to Refilwe, "your bones and your whole body get old." He had asked Refilwe to lead him there with his bundle of bones and potions, made from herbs and objects known only to himself. She made the fire for him under the black three legged potjie pot, half filled it with water she had scooped up from a stream they had crossed and left him, promising to come and fetch him at sunrise.

She knew he would throw the bones, mix his concoctions, and communicate with the spirits until he knew the answers to his questions.

She turned round to look at him one last time, the swirling mist making the scene look as if he were floating in the air, a weightless being from another world.

Refilwe saw him in silhouette before she called out to him. "I am here my husband, ready to take you back to our home" She emptied the now cold pot and filled it with his potions, wrapped them all in the blanket and lifted them onto her head. They did not speak on the way back home. Shaka went to sit under the flame tree and called for Zenze. "My son, our ancestors came to me in my dreams. They made me understand that you are going to go on a long trip, but something is puzzling me. They talked of a cave and a box and I am confused." Zenze hung his head and said, "I know of such a box and cave," and told Shaka what had happened on the night he found Jamie and where he had hidden the box. "You have not done a terrible deed, my son, you just did what you thought was right at the time. I too would probably have done just that. I think now is the time to go and fetch the box and see what secrets lie inside."

"Come and look for berries with me Zenze," said Jamie. "Temba is busy beading, and does not want to join me. She is calling me an irritating mosquito again!"

"I can't, I have to go somewhere on my own."

"Are you going to meet a girl at the river?" chuckled Jamie wickedly.

"No, Temba is right you are an irritating mosquito,

I am going on an errand for my father and must do so without a buzzing in my ear all the time. Go and find Kabo, he is always ready to eat, especially berries. Jamie looked at Zenze in a questioning manner, he knew something different was afoot but knew better than to probe any deeper. "You are coming back aren't you?"

Zenze looked at him in a peculiar way and then said, "I have to go and speak to my father." Zenze found Shaka leaning on the rock wall that surrounded the sheep enclosure, sightlessly gazing into the distance. "Father," he said "I think that I should take Mfana with me to the caves as he so needs to learn about surviving in the wild. Also, seeing as the box is part of his life, I think it only fair that he comes with me. I know he can be a nuisance and a hindrance, but he is growing into a brave boy and I would like him to come with me."

"I knew from the day you were born that you would be an understanding chief one day, replied Shaka. "You keep showing me that you care for other people's feelings and that you are a decision maker. I know you love Mfana as a brother, and will guide and love him and protect him from all dangers. Yes, I think you are right – take him with you. We need to find out the secrets of the box before we decide what to do."

Zenze did not have to go and find Jamie, he knew that sooner or later Jamie would come looking for him, in the meantime he began preparations for his cave trip. He needed light to see in the cave so went looking for his mom. He asked her whether she had any bits and pieces of cloth he could use and some animal fat to make torches. She knew that boys loved to be out in the dark and needed torches so she showed him an old sack full of old cloths and then took him behind a lean-to where she stored her cooking fat in a large tin.

Zenze put some fat into a pot and hung it over the embers of the fire that was kept going all day. He wanted the fat to melt so that he could soak the cloths with it. He went into the surrounding woods to look for some straight branches and monkey twine, hearing Jamie before he saw him because he was not the quietest of walkers! Zenze made a mental note to himself that he needed to teach Jamie about walking quietly through the forest.

"Can I help you with whatever you are doing"? asked Jamie in that younger brother voice, so full of 'wanting-to-please-you' tone. "I thought you were going somewhere."

"I have a surprise for you, you are coming with me

to explore some caves, just you and me." Jamie was so thrilled he jumped into the air shouting, "yay, yay, when do we leave?"

"Not so fast, whirlwind, we need to prepare. In case you don't know, it is very dark in caves with strange monsters and animals in them," said Zenze in a wobbly, scary kind of voice. "We need torches and I am looking for some straight branches and monkey twine. If you are afraid you don't have to come," he teased.

"I'm not afraid of the dark," answered Jamie with more bravado than he felt. They found six straight branches and lots of monkey twine and walked back to the fire. Zenze showed Jamie how to dip the cloths into the fat, wrap them around the straight branch and then tie them firmly with the monkey rope, all the while giving Jamie bits and pieces of information in reply to the dozens of questions he was being asked. Yes, he had been in the cave before, no, there were no monsters that he knew of. Yes, it would be very dark but some filtered light could be seen. Yes, he knew exactly why they were going – to collect a box. No he did not know what was inside it. He skirted around telling him the story of the box. They worked companionably, cross legged in front of the pot of fat, Jamie occasionally flicking the odd bit of fat in

Zenze's direction. The shadows lengthened, they heard the herd boys coming back from the pasture, coaxing the cows back into the boma (shelter) for the night, flicking their whips over their heads, shouting 'yoh, yoh, yoh'.

"Tomorrow we need to prepare for our journey. It's not going to be a long journey but you might as well start learning how to survive in the wild, you never know when you might need it." said Zenze. Jamie took Gerbi out of his pocket and began to scratch him behind the ears while offering him some pumpkin seeds he took from his other pocket. "Do you hear, Gerbi? We are going on an adventure and of course you are coming as well." A wild rustling in the trees overhead and a shower of leaves announced Xixi who landed beside Jamie and then hugged him around the neck. "Did you hear Xixi, isn't that exciting? We are going on a trip to some caves. You don't need to be afraid." Jamie knew that Xixi could be very afraid of strange places, but as long as he was clutched to Jamie's neck he would be fine.

"You are going to have to think not only for yourself, but Gerbi and Xixi as well," said Zenze, as he arranged all the torches in a pile. "You are going to be responsible for their safety and wellbeing on this trip, don't rely on me. Look at this trip as a 'growing-up-trip'. You are always telling me how grown up you are and how clever you are, now is the time to start showing me that this is really the case." A loud clanging made them stop in their bantering and smile, it was time to eat and Refilwe was calling them by hitting on a pot. Holding Xixi by the hand, Gerbi in his other hand, Jamie made his way to a large drum of water to wash his hands.

Zenze put his arm on his shoulder and said, "you did well today, Mfana, I am going to make you into a tracker and warrior yet." Jamie's grin was proof that there is no food tastier than praise. Xixi washed his face as well, splashing water all around him and Gerbi daintily washed behind his ears.

They approached the fire where Shaka and Refilwe were already sitting. Temba ladled some marogo over the 'pap', white corn meal and Jamie and Zenze, sitting cross-legged ate hungrily from the communal pot with their fingers. Xixi ate the little scraps Jamie fed him, and Gerbi continued to break and eat the pumpkin seeds at Jamie's feet.

"You two have a lot of preparation to do tomorrow, I think you need a good night's sleep," said Shaka.

"Where are you going," immediately chirped Temba who had silently joined the family circle.

"No girls allowed this time," said Zenze, "Jamie and I are going to visit some caves and I thought it would be good to go, just us boys, don't be upset. If we think it is worth it, we'll take you another time."

"You can do some beading, tomorrow," whispered Refilwe and Temba looked at her with big eyes swimming in pools of liquid. Sometimes she wished she was a boy. She could be free to wander wherever she liked, go away on adventures like those two were going on tomorrow and not have to do beadwork, or learn to cook or keep the huts tidy. 'Unfair, unfair, unfair,' she thought, the eternal complaint of the teenager. Everyone faded to their respective huts, each one with thoughts only known to themselves.

CHAPTER II

....I too was young once...

amie was dreaming of rolling down a waterfall when he heard Zenze laugh. Zenze had pulled the blanket from Jamie and in doing so he had rolled off the bedding and landed with Xixi on his head. "Get up you sleepy head we have many things to prepare and you have been sleeping all night already! Breakfast is waiting." Jamie pulled on his trousers, feeling for Gerbi and headed out to wash his face and hands before breakfast. He put Gerbi on the edge of the bowl "I don't know how you know to wash behind your ears, but you do!" teased Jamie. "Sorry little Gerbi, you probably wanted to sleep a little longer."

Refilwe ladled some soft porridge into a gourd and poured milk over it, handing it to Jamie saying, "learn well, little warrior, your life is just beginning and it is a long and hard journey to become a man. Learn from Zenze and he in turn will learn from you." Gerbi, from his perch on Jamie's shoulder, ran down his arm and nibbled at the porridge. Xixi had run into the bushes as soon as he scampered out of the hut, probably just to stretch his limbs and do his toileting. He now shared some porridge with Jamie getting it all over his face. Jamie laughed and said, "first stream we come to, you'll have to wash yourself Xixi, else other animals might think you are a white-faced ghost with all that porridge sticking to your face!"

"Goway, goway" called the two loeries in the Acacia trees and Refilwe knew that these two birds would follow the boys. How did she know? She just did. She was a mother!

"Let's think of where we are going and what kind of covering we need for our bodies. Caves can be cold and damp, so I think we need to bring a blanket. Remember to roll up your blanket and have it ready when we start our journey. Unless there is light coming in from somewhere, caves are very dark, but we do not know this, so, we need light and that is why we were making torches yesterday."

"OK, but how are we going to light them?" asked Jamie, something stirred in his memory about lighting a fire, but no sooner had he thought about it that it was gone.

"We are going to have to bring some hot, red coals

with us, without burning ourselves."

"Oh yes? this I have got to see." Jamie knew what an important part of life in the village it was to keep a fire burning all through the night. The red hot embers could be used to start the first fire of the next day.

"Just before we leave, we'll place some red coals in this clay pot with a handle and take it with us. We'll wrap it in a blanket and keep an eye on it so that it does not burn the blanket or us."

"That's smart, but dangerous," said Jamie," is there no easier way to start a fire?

"Yes, you could rub two sticks together until you had a spark, but you, little bug, would take half a day to do so."

"No, No, I know there is another way, but I cannot remember."

"Our father was given some magic sticks that make fire, but he keeps them hidden and will certainly not give them to us, besides you're in training to be a warrior, and must learn to do things the way our ancestors did."

"Ok", said Jamie, with a frown and his eyes hundreds of miles away his mind trying to remember another world, another time, another life. Something was nagging him about making a fire.

"Mfana, we must really work on your walking through the bush. Anyone could hear you from the other side of the forest, you walk like a rhino on the rampage. You need to learn to walk noiselessly, not an easy feat. We could be walking close to animals so you need to know a few facts. You must try to become part of the bush so that no animal will know you are there. We might meet dangerous animals, maybe hungry ones and then you need to have your wits about you. Always be aware of the direction of the wind, because it is better to be downwind from an animal, in other words, in a position where the wind is blowing away from the animal towards you, because, if you are upwind, the animal will smell your scent.

"On this trip to the caves, we are going to pretend to be hunters stalking animals, so we are going to walk in a crouching position. Sometimes we may need to crawl on our hands and knees, or, you may have to 'leopard crawl'. You've seen how the other boys in the village practice, and you have as well, going down on your stomach and pulling yourself forward with your elbows. Most important, move slowly and do not make any sudden movements, especially, little Rhino, be careful where you place your feet when you are near an animal. No stepping on dry twigs or leaves and no shouting 'yes' and punching the air when you see something interesting."

"I'm listening," said Jamie.

"I think we must decide on a sound, a bird call perhaps to call each other, in that way we'll blend with nature and be able to keep in touch with each other.

"I know", shouted Jamie, "I want to make the 'krik, krik, krik, sound."

"That's a good one," Zenze smiled "seeing as the *mousebird* is rather a clumsy flier because of its long and untidy tail and often crashes into bushes when landing – just like you!"

"That's it then, our call to each other will be the mousebird's call."

"Ok, Mfana, but if we are in danger we need another call. During the day, the hooting of an *owl* would be out of place, so that's what we should use. You know the call of that owl, the one with the ear tufts and the orange eyes. It makes a sound like an insect almost, 'prrrpt, prrrpt', practice it, let me hear" Jamie mimiced the sound 'prrrpt,

prrrpt' 'prrrpt, prrrpt'. He and Zenze give each other a 'high five'.

"How we are going to control Xixi is another thing. This trip is going to be so good for him as well, I am sure he will easily copy our behavior. What you have to learn, will come naturally to him, who knows, he might come in useful. He will probably climb from tree to tree and swing here, there and everywhere, always keeping us in his sight. He is so part of nature that he will go unnoticed."

"Zenze, you said we would have to bring food, which makes me to wonder when we are going to eat. Look, even that *lizard* is waiting for a morsel," and before he could even realize what he was saying, the words rolled off his tongue.

'Lizard, lizard why do you stare

In the sun's strong glare

Are you waiting for an ant

Or perhaps an elephant?

See your tongue dart like an arrow

No, you don't – you cannot eat a sparrow.'

"Did you teach me that Zenze?"

"I might have, if I had known it, but I have not heard

it before. You are becoming stranger by the day, Mfana, I wonder what you are going to remember next. Let's go and see what our mother has prepared for us, she will help us with what kind of food we need to take on our trip." Zenze realized Jamie's memory was coming back to him. Someone had taught him that rhyme and it certainly wasn't anyone in the village. In fact it wasn't until a little while ago that he was known as Mfana, until one day he had said, "Jamie, I am Jamie."

Refilwe had been watching the preparations from afar and heard snatches of their conversation. She knew the excitement that was mounting in their young hearts, especially Jamie, and she was pleased. She understood the lure of a first taste of freedom and adventure for children on the cusp of young adulthood. She sighed and thought, 'why do children want to rush childhood, when it is the most magic time of their lives, and so short?'

"Mama, do you have anything for us to take on our trip to the caves"?

"Yes, I can suggest dry biltong, we have some that is just dry enough and I can let you have some dry *mopane* worms as well."

"Mmmmm" said Jamie .

"Jamie, do you remember when we first offered you mopane worms? You actually said, "no, no, no, I cannot eat caterpillars." I explained that all the green 'guts' had been squeezed out of them and that when dried they tasted of nuts. You took your time to start enjoying them. It is excellent food to take on a journey. They keep for months and have enough fat in them to give you energy. For two energetic young boys who are going to explore caves, I think they are a very necessary food. You will be able to find berries to eat and there are clear, pure streams on the way, so you won't need to carry much water. Bring a sharp knife, you always need one."

Jamie had been looking at her with awe. "How do you know all this?"

"Do you think that I have lived in this kraal all my life and do not know about the caves? Do you think that I was never a young girl and never wanted adventure, like you? I know children think their parents have never been young, do you think we were born old? Silly boy, of course I know where the caves are, and yes I did go into them, only once and not very far into them as I am afraid of the dark. I saw you making torches yesterday and that is very wise." Refilwe pretended to shiver and whispered, "I hate the bats that live in those caves."

"So, you are afraid of the caves and the bats as well?" asked Jamie cheekily.

"Well, cheeky boy, if you must know I should have said the eyes and smell of the bats. You'll see what I mean when you are in the caves. I wonder what Xixi and Gerbi are going to think. You are going to take them with you, aren't you? I don't want to look after those two. I'm asking because I know that often children want pets, but after a while it's the parents who have to look after them. I must tell you though, Jamie, I am very proud of the way you look after Xixi and Gerbi. Because I have seen how responsibly you look after your pets, I feel I can trust you to look after yourself and it shows me that you are leaving childhood behind and heading towards young adulthood." Jamie felt ten feet tall.

Zenze walked off, saying he needed to ask Nelson to do his chores for him while he was away and Jamie sauntered off in the direction of some sugar cane fields. He wanted to cut some sugar cane to take on the journey as he loved gnawing at the stalk and tasting the sweetness. He knew that Xixi and Gerbi would also enjoy a treat of sugar cane and keep them out of mischief for a while. Jamie felt so excited he was almost trembling. He could not wait for tomorrow morning when they would head out towards the caves. He needed this afternoon to make a long cord for Gerbi and with these thoughts in mind he fantasized how exciting the adventure would be. Little did he know that tomorrow would be a turning point in his life.

CHAPTER 12

....Wake up, Mfana

ist, looking like monsters changing shape, ebbed and waved across the kraal. An eerie silence, as if it were a mantle wrapping itself around the kraal, hung over the valley as Zenze shook Jamie awake. "Wake up Mfana, it's time to go on our adventure, or are you too afraid?" Jamie sprung out of his sleeping blanket, rolled it up, added the long cord and slipped on his trousers. Xixi, rubbed his eyes and already heading for the outdoors, scratched himself and made his 'xi,xi' noises, annoyed and confused at being woken up so early in the morning. Jamie touched his mother on her cheek and said. "See you soon. I am leaving with Zenze." She touched his hand sleepily and gave it a squeeze. That was all he needed. Holding his rolled up blanket, Gerbi in his pocket, he walked towards the fire and watched as Zenze, using two long sticks, placed three red hot coals

in a clay bowl that had been buried into a bigger bowl lined with wet clay. The larger bowl had a handle and a cover and Zenze carefully wrapped his blanket around it before strapping it to his back. The only sounds to be heard were the odd bark of a dog, rudely awakened from his sleep. A tiny squirrel showed up, keeping his distance but checking out Zenze and Jamie, tail upright, whiskers flicking, while Jamie stretched, yawned and drank in the early morning sounds of the bush. He smiled as he saw the slight movement to his right. It was 'Ruga' the largest of the many *tortoises* that lived in the kraal, moving at its own sweet pace. The tortoises were an integral part of every child born in the kraal, a first playmate, a beloved pet. Jamie remembers touching Ruga's hard shell for the first time and being fascinated by the scaly head that peeped from under its shell. Jamie was able to observe all the indentations, markings and scaly legs of the tortoise because Ruga was a very slow mover. He could identify all the other tortoises but Ruga was his favorite. "See you later Ruga, I'm going on an adventure."

Zenze and Jamie moved towards the river, down a path that they knew well, but this time Zenze took a sharp left turn into the side of a hill and they started climbing a zigzag path that was known as 'eeinabene', or sore legs path. "Let's go, little brother, are those skinny legs strong enough for the climb?" Jamie had been along this path so often he knew it by heart, but the early morning mist made shapes differ, distorting them and the feeling that they were being followed would not leave him. They walked in silence, alert and so full of excitement their hearts beat faster, the mist so dense they could hardly see each other. He hoped the occasional crashing of branches close to him was Xixi moving from tree to tree and the sporadic rustling at ground level, the sounds of little creatures, rodents and lizards that had escaped the nocturnal predators. Little by little the mist rose until they could see more clearly; the boulders no longer looked like moving beasts and the shapes that had looked like monsters trying to claw Jamie, now looked like trees. Zenze knew Jamie must be feeling very excited, yet a little afraid. He remembered how nervous he had felt on his first early morning outing, so he tried out their signal, 'krikkk, krikkk, krikkk' and mouthed a silent "yes" when he heard the reply 'krikkk, krikkk, krikkk'.

Zenze in particular was anxious because he felt the responsibility towards Jamie resting heavily on his shoulders, not only because he was older but because of the unknown impact the box and its contents would have on Jamie's life. He wondered what they would find in the box.

The track, riddled with boulders and loose stones was difficult to climb and now and again he slipped a little. Obviously, from the sounds behind him, Jamie was doing the same. Up, up, up they hiked and at one stage, Jamie said, "Stop! Zenze, I'm running out of breath, let's stop and rest for a while, I need a drink of water." They both knew how important it is to keep drinking water while on a long hike. Sitting on a boulder, overlooking a most magnificent gorge, enormous boulders of hardened volcanic larva protruding like huge growths on a dragon's skin, climbing plants clinging to some of the surfaces like an unkempt beard, they ate a banana. Xixi peeled his banana like an expert, peeling each segment of skin down to a point where he could hold it until the last bite. Jamie shared some of his with Gerbi and let him run up and down the protea bush they were sitting under, twirling the end of the string around his middle finger. "Gerbi is quite a character" said Zenze, "I think you have trained him well because you've treated him firmly but lovingly I have never seen you being cruel to him, like I've seen some nasty boys beating dogs and other animals to make them do tricks."

"When I was given Gerbi, my friend Nelson said that to tame an animal, or for that matter, to make and keep friends one has to be patient, understanding of our differences and above all have respect for each other. I didn't understand at first, but then he taught me about Gerbi's habits, his likes and dislikes, the way that nature has made him special and different from any other animal. I learnt that, like humans, animals too are different from each other and some things can change but others just cannot. Gerbi is a gerbil and I cannot make him into a monkey, just as I cannot make Xixi into a human – even though he would like to be one! Wouldn't you?" said Jamie as he gently tugged Xixi's tail and lovingly scratched his back.

"Let's move on again," said Zenze, "if we rest too long it will be more difficult to start again as our muscles will cool down and hurt even more." "Up, up, up" moaned Jamie, "does this hill ever end?" As they hiked higher the vegetation grew more sparse and drier and the flowering proteas ranging in colour from deep bright reds to purples to vivid orange looked like dollops of brilliant paint on a green, yellow and blue canvas. The path took a steep dip and they felt their muscles pulling as they scrambled down over loose stones, holding on to protruding roots and bushes to keep their balance. Again there was a change in vegetation, now greener and lush and the sound of water louder.

They entered a narrow ravine, the mountain face, rugged and menacing, looming over them. On closer inspection small wild flowers grew from the rock as if suspended in the air. Jamie wondered aloud, "how on earth do those flowers manage to grow in between rocks, when there must be so little soil for their roots". "Isn't it strange, Mfana, that weeds grow anywhere and with so little help from the earth, whereas humans have to work hard, tilling the soil and feeding it for crops to grow. I know that when you were little, you used to hate the smell of cow dung, but you soon learnt what a wonderful fertilizer for the crops it is. After all, the cows are just giving back to nature what they eat – grass!"

"Talking of manure, you know what really amazed me, was when our mother smoothed hot cow dung on the floor of our huts. I just could not believe it and yet now I see what a very good floor covering it turns out to be. "Uffa!" I was so annoyed when she asked me to help her.

"I think you are getting your memory back," Mfana, you are using words I don't know. The other day you were annoyed at the wind blowing sand in your eyes and you said 'uffa' as well".

"I think I am remembering more and more Zenze, I am becoming very aware of another language I spoke. Words and pieces of songs keep jumping into my head." Sunlight filtered through the canopy of trees and just as Jamie's stomach began to growl from hunger, they heard the sound of the rippling stream before they saw it.

"Let's stop for something to eat at the stream." Almost on cue, Xixi landed on Jamie's shoulder and Jamie laughingly said, "come here you white-faced monkey, come and have your face washed before you frighten all the animals away. The longer that porridge sticks to your fur, the harder it will be to wash off!" Jamie led him by the hand and Xixi, head lowered as if he was going to be punished allowed Jamie to pour water over his head and body. "You always give me a tough time when you need your head washed, but you know it is necessary otherwise all that mess on your face will attract bugs and insects," said Jamie as he gently rubbed the porridge off his face. Zenze turned his gaze away and smiled, remembering a little boy who screamed and kicked when he needed a bath saying he was clean and didn't need to wash, especially his hair! How time was flying and history repeating itself!

As they sat on a big rock, feet dangling in the stream a *fish eagle* sat patiently waiting for the right moment to dive into the water and catch an unsuspecting fish, its black flight feathers and chestnut underbelly gleaming in the sun. "Zenze, I think that eagle is hungry too, look at how his eyes are concentrating on the surface of the water. At that moment the eagle swooped low and plucked a fish out of the water with its claws. The boys were stunned at this impressive show.

"Jamie, look on the other side, there, amongst those reeds see those very small birds with magnificent colors! They are bee-eaters."

"These are the birds that don't make nests in trees but in burrows in sandbanks, aren't they?" chirped Jamie.

"Yes, do you remember when you were this little?",

he said, showing a height by turning his hand palm up in the African manner, "we went out looking for tadpoles at the river near our home. You heard such a loud twittering you kept on looking up into the trees, while you should have been looking at the sandbank where thousands of bee-eaters were making their 'terk,terk' call. You were so interested that you forgot all about the tadpoles and wanted to count the bee-eaters instead. Of course you know who had to fish for the tadpoles in the end? As usual! I remember how you watched those tadpoles every day, until they grew legs, lost their tails and became frogs. I also remember a little boy who cried when they were released back into the river. We had to have a farewell ceremony."

"Talking of frogs, look at those *herons* wading in the water looking for frogs with their submerged beaks. Zenze gives Jamie a piece of bread and they companionably tear bits off and chew, kicking the water.

All of a sudden, something is not quite right. It is too quiet. The herons have moved away, the bee-eaters have disappeared into their burrows, Xixi is sitting very close to Jamie, and Gerbi has crept under Jamie's chin. Squinting his eyes and following the winding course of the river, Zenze noticed that even the bees that were buzzing in and around the reed flowers had moved away. Has he lost his sense of smell all of a sudden? Why can't he smell the slightly pungent smell of dampness and trodden grass that one always smells near water? Jamie makes sniffing sounds and almost turns green with nausea when he inhales an overpowering, disgusting smell. Gagging and pinching his nose, Jamie looks at Zenze, eyes wide. He feels his food begin to make its way up inside him. That dreadful smell hits him like a punch in the face, and then dissipates into the air. Did he imagine it? If it were a dead animal, wouldn't the smell still hang in the air? He knows he must get out of this place. He feels evil around him and he is afraid. A word jumps into Jamie's head, 'Tiki?'

"Zenze, something is not right – I can just feel it, and that horrible smell! I smelt it one day when I was out with Temba at the swimming pond – I don't like it here, let's move from here. I feel something nasty around us." Silently and quickly packing away their belongings they started up the path on the other side of the stream. The path at first muddy and slippery with moss growing on boulders alongside it, gradually became drier, the grasses bordering it small and spiky. The canopy of trees grew less thick and the sunrays weakly warmed their arms.

Again they climbed higher with Jamie repeating every so often "up, up, up will this hill never end?" "We are nearly there 'grumbler', see that mass of rocks to the left, the entrance to the cave is somewhere there on the side you cannot see from here. They trudged along in silence, Xixi swinging from branch to branch and Gerbi clinging to Jamie's shoulder. They were walking through a large field of veld grass, almost as tall as Jamie when from nowhere, a slightly stinky smelling wind enveloped them, flattening the grass around them as if a giant boulder were being rolled around them. Goose bumps crept up Zenze and Jamie's arms, Gerbi scuttled back into the protection of Jamie's pocket and Jamie cried out, "if it's you evil Tiki, show yourself you foul smelling thing. I'm not afraid of you"

Just as suddenly, the wind abated and a flock of about twenty *pipits* lifted noisily out of the tall grass, their clear 'chrrp-chereeo' call easing the tension. "We must have come very close to some of their nests, for them to make such a noise, but I wonder" said Zenze in a hushed voice, "I wonder."

CHAPTER 13

....make your mousebird call...

hey skirted the huge, boulder strewn outcrop and as they came round to the shaded side, Jamie felt a thrill of anticipation. Xixi already boulder hopping and jumping, making his 'xi xi' sounds, his long arms touching the floor bounced up and down. As he looked at Xixi, out of nowhere a rhyme formed in Jamie's mind 'no more monkeys jumping on the bed', but he was so looking forward to finding the entrance that he forgot about it as soon as he thought about it.

"Jamie, stop!" shouted Zenze. "Look on top of that big stone, call Xixi back immediately, there's a snake". Jamie made a 'click, click' sound with his tongue and the monkey came running, leaping onto his shoulder.

"Where? where? I can't see anything," whispered Jamie.

125

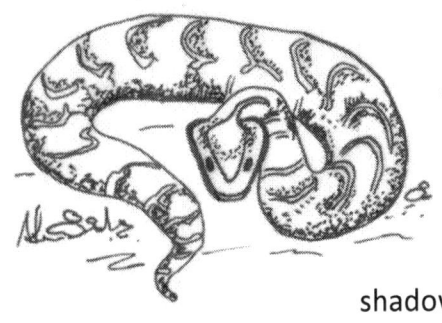

"It's a snake, a *puffadder* and he is so camouflaged he blends in with the color of the rocks. "There, in the shadow of that overhanging rock. Look closely at the black markings on his brownish yellow body and especially notice his head that is shaped like an arrow, with narrow neck. Its bite is very poisonous and you should never try to go too close to it because it spits venom into your eyes. He is not annoyed at the moment, but if he were, he would rear its head and strike. You cannot mess around with a puffadder because he does not give way when startled. He will stand his ground, puff and hiss before striking, that's why he is called a 'puff' adder." Xixi screamed and covered his eyes, not wanting to see the snake and Gerbi trembled quietly in Jamie's pocket. "Zenze, please let's find the entrance to that cave, I've got a jumping stomach and I want to get away from that snake."

"Let's move along, Jamie, it's getting late and I am undecided about when to enter the caves. I think we should make camp close to the entrance and then start exploring the caves starting early in the morning. Let's find a place to make a fire and sleep under the stars." Zenze chose a place where he noticed someone had previously made a fire. The ground was free of any bushes and stones that might hide something dangerous.

Zenze immediately sent Jamie to look for small dry twigs but reminded him, "don't go too far, always stay where I can see you, or give me our mousebird call often." Soon Jamie returned with a fair amount of small twigs and dragged a larger branch behind him. Zenze blew on the coals in the clay pot until he saw a spark and added the small dry twigs. As soon as the twigs caught alight he gently tipped them onto the ground, surrounded by the larger branches that Jamie had broken. He tended the fire, blowing onto it occasionally, until it was large and comforting. "There, that's a good fire and should keep any animals away. Let's see what we have to eat."

"Before we eat, a good hunter makes sure that his fire is burning well, his surroundings secure and his bedroll free of insects. Sweep around the fire and lay out our blankets, then hang up anything we don't need right now onto the end of a branch so no creepy crawlies can get to them." They each broke a branch and Jamie copied Zenze's sweeping motions until not even a tiny leaf lay on the ground. Zenze took some cooked corn cobs and biltong (dry strips of meat) from his back pack and placed them on a rock. "Come and wash your hands, Mfana" said Zenze as he held a gourd filled with water ready to pour over Jamie's hands.

"Don't you dare tell me to remember to wash my hands before eating, again. I am a young warrior now and know that it is absolutely important to do so." Zenze lifted his eyebrows and thought that Jamie was acting very grown up and wondered how long it would last?

They sat cross legged and while Jamie ate a bit of corn and then some dried meat biltong, Zenze finished first his corn and then his biltong. Jamie noticed this and remarked, "Zenze, why do you not mix your foods? I have often seen you eat first one food and then the other, whereas I like to take a bite of the dried meat biltong and then a bite of the corn."

Because I choose to do so, because we are all different. It is neither right nor wrong. Well, as an example, we African people are quite comfortable eating with our hands, but I know that other people aren't."

"I used to eat with a knife and fork," blurted Jamie. "Zenze, I'm remembering, I'm remembering".

"Mfana, I know you are a fountain of knowledge, but at the moment I am so tired I can hardly keep my eyes open. Lets hang our bags on a branch and please go to sleep!" Knife and fork? thought Zenze, whatever next would this boy think of!

Xixi had finished his corn and was already curled on Jamie's blanket while Gerbi cleaned his little face of the few bits of corn left on it. Jamie put him in his pocket, making sure the cord was firmly attached. He curled up on his blanket with his mind racing in all directions. He was remembering another language and another world but there were so many gaps missing.

It was full moon and a hyena laughed in the dark. The birds that had been twittering earlier on were now silent, and it seemed as if the whole world was going to sleep. All of a sudden, a noise Jamie could not identify became louder and louder. "Zenze, Zenze" he shook half-asleep Zenze awake – "what is happening?"

Zenze was immediately awake and listening. He silently made waving motions and big eyes and said, "*bats*, it's the bats leaving the caves from their special entrance for their nightly feeding. The sound you hear is the sound of their wings. Don't look at me with such big frightened eyes – they don't eat children, they eat insects and fruit." Jamie could see a few stragglers and grimaced, "they are so ugly and so noisy, their high-pitched sound is drilling into my ears."

Zenze had to laugh at this young brother, who dramatized every occurrence. "Bats don't find their food by sight but rather by their sense of hearing and smell. Those high- pitched sounds you hear 'echo' or 'bounce off', an insect, and that is how they know where to find it. Some people think that bats are blind but they are not, they just don't see as well as they hear. Yes, I agree they are ugly with wings for arms, small eyes and long tongues, but did you know that they are the only mammal that can fly?"

"Mammal?" asked Jamie.

"A bat does not lay an egg like a chicken, its babies are born alive from its body. That's why it is called a mammal, animals that have live births are called mammals. A baby bat is called a pup. Can we please go to sleep now?"

Jamie was still a little frightened and looked for Xixi to cuddle and realized the little monkey had slept through the noise. 'Of course', thought Jamie, 'he is cleverer than me, he knows a lot more about wild life than I do. If he is not worried, I won't be either', and with that he curled onto his blanket, covered himself and fell fast asleep to dream of caves, knives, forks, bats and again something familiar, at the edge of his dream, beckoned him, but in the morning he remembered nothing. Dreams have a habit of doing that.

CHAPTER 14

….but it's so dark…

enze woke up with a start, Jamie was standing over him and Xixi was jumping around his head. "What's happening, what's wrong?" He could not believe his eyes, the bags were down from the branches and Jamie, with a big grin on his face was ready to go. "I am just too excited to sleep any longer, come on lazy brother, the sun is up and the caves are waiting." Jamie handed Zenze some berries he'd collected and the four of them ate them with some bread. Jamie had blown into the fire to get it going again and lined the cloth torches next to it – hoping to impress Zenze.

Zenze seriously said "Jamie, there are some rules you must keep when in the caves. You cannot go doing your own thing in there because I will lose you forever. I know you are adventurous and want to explore the caves any old how, but you must promise me to not go exploring on your own. Remember last night we spoke about right and wrong and making choices, well, in a cave there are right and wrong ways to behave and that is that. The darkness in a cave is total, which means you can see absolutely nothing, not even your hand in front of your eyes, so our torches are very important. You need to keep them dry and alight at all costs. The walls of caves are often damp, so don't brush your torch against them. Walk slowly, feel where you are walking and don't forget your head as the roof can be low with bits of rock pointing down. Water dripping from the ceiling of a cave, drop by drop, for years and years, forms these rock formations that at times can look like giant teeth."

"Jamie, you must stay close to me at all times so we will tie ourselves together with some rope. Sounds echo in caves and seem louder than what they really are, so, no shouting unless absolutely necessary. Remember our special bird call, use it, in that way we'll keep in contact with each other. Keep Xixi and Gerbi tied to you as well. Leave the fire burning and lets go and find the opening to the cave, then we'll come back, light the torches and start exploring."

They walked towards the rocky outcrop that looked like an old bearded man's scraggy face, the green, soft foliage on top like a frilly hat. What impressed Jamie the most were the vertical scars in the rock face that looked like tear marks. "What sad looking rocks," he observed, "I hope they are not unhappy that we are going to visit them."

"You really say odd things sometimes" retorted Zenze.

They skirted the base of the outcrop and Zenze whispered, "we're nearly there, I'll give you a clue – the opening is about twice my height above us. See if you can find it. Don't think it is going to be simple, don't think there will be a track or anything obvious, because this is a sacred site, known only to our tribe and not many people come here. Our father Shaka used to come here quite often, when he could still see, and, it was he who took me my first time. - He too made me look for the entrance."

Xixi was already scuttling over the boulders, looking for whatever monkeys look for amongst boulders. As Gerbi's head peeped out of Jamie's pocket, he stopped to attach the very long cord he'd carried over his shoulder to Gerbi's shorter cord – he did not want to lose him in the caves. "OK, young warrior, lead the way. If you move too far from the entrance I'll say 'cold'. If you are going in the right direction I will say 'warm' then 'warmer', and when you are absolutely right I'll say 'hot'. You know how we have played that game before. They walked upwards for a while and Jamie turned right towards some boulders but Zenze said 'cold', so he turned left. Jamie had a short stick and prodded and poked the vegetation, dislodging small stones and the odd lizard. They walked past the bush that covered the entrance and Jamie prodded it a little too high and missed the opening. Zenze let Jamie walk a bit more and then said 'cold'. 'Uffa' hissed Jamie, how could I have missed it?"

"Don't give up. Look closely for signs." Jamie looked at the bush and saw that a small branch had leaves that were almost dead, and thought it could have been because someone had been here a while ago and broken the branch. He was about to rip the bush aside when Zenze held up his hand to stop him.

"Stop, Jamie. Yes, you have found the entrance but do you want everyone else to do so as well? Just as you saw the dry little branch, if you had to break more branches, anyone else scouting around the area could find it. Don't be impatient and rash. Let's go and fetch our belongings and come back with our lit torches." Jamie thought he would burst with excitement and scrambled back to the campsite, Xixi felt Jamie's excitement and started doing cartwheels.

Again they put some red embers into the clay pot and Zenze strapped it to his back with a thick blanket to protect him from the heat. They made sure the fire was doused, sprinkled sand on it and turned towards the cave entrance. At the entry to the cave, Zenze showed Jamie how to carefully move the bush away from the entrance and Jamie gave a gasp when he saw the small opening.

"Mfana, we are going to have to crawl on our stomach for a little while, then the cave opens up and we'll be able to stand. I'll light one of the torches then. Don't be afraid because there will be a sliver of light coming in from an opening somewhere in the cave. Keep Xixi on your back and Gerbi in your pocket." Zenze lay down and began leopard crawling through the hole, Jamie, with Xixi on his back began to lie down, but at the last moment, remembered to tie the end of the long cord he had around Gerbi to the bottom of the bush and followed Zenze down the tunnel. He felt the tug of the cord unraveling from around his shoulder.

Jamie felt as if he could not breathe, he felt his heart beat drumming in his ears, but was comforted by the sound of Zenze's body scraping on the floor ahead of him. Xixi, petrified, clung to his back like a leech. After a short while, their eyes grew accustomed to the dark and they began to see a glimmer of light. Jamie was aware of the sides of the tunnel close to him. He could touch the damp stone face closest to him. "Krikk, krikk, krikk", he whispered, but he was so tense, the sound stuck in his throat and it came out as a guttural sound, "kkkk,kkk,kkkk." He tried again and before he could finish, heard the answering call from Zenze. The sound was right up close to him and in that instant he bumped into something soft that chuckled. Relieved, he knew it was Zenze.

"How are you feeling?" asked Zenze? "You can stand up now. Are Gerbi and Xixi still with you?"

"Yes, but this is so eerie, I have never known such darkness and even though I cannot see around me, I can feel a void around me. I am not sure I like being here, Zenze, please light that torch."

He heard muffled sounds, it was Zenze muttering to himself and then he caught a glimpse of the red coals and soon after a lit torch. His relief was enormous but now there was an added scary aspect – shadows. The flames on the torch produced scary, multi-shaped shadows that made everything appear to move and jump - he wanted to turn around and run. Zenze put his arm around him and the shaking Xixi. "Your eyes will become accustomed to the dark, don't be afraid of the shadows, there is nothing and no one here but us." He planted the torch into some damp earth, made Jamie sit down next to it and said. "We came to find a box and that is what I am going to do. While you wait for me, look there on that rock and you'll see some drawings of animals. They were done many, many years ago by the people who came here for shelter or to hide from other warriors."

Jamie scrunched up his eyes and could barely make out the drawings that looked like cows and buck and other animals he could not recognize. He kept on thinking about the darkness. He tried to remember what Refilwe had told him about the caves. The smell and ooh! the bats. "Zenze, the smell in here is really bad, I suppose it's the bats?" asked Jamie hopefully, Zenze did not reply, he obviously had not heard. He looked up and to his horror saw many little red eyes. "Please, please don't go away, Zenze, I'm really afraid here. There are too many little red, evil eyes looking at me"

"I'm right here, just to the right of you and I have found the box". Zenze slipped the little red tractor into the bag he had around his neck and picked up the box and in doing so, put his foot down at an angle, twisting his ankle, falling down from the pain. As he lost his balance, he put out his hand, and the torch flew from his grip, clattering against the damp wall and fizzling out with a ssssssssss. "Oh no! Oh no! Etshuwi! Etshuwi! Etshuwi! Ouch! Ouch! Ouch! exclaimed Zenze, "I don't believe this is happening."

"What, what has happened Zenze?" Jamie asked in a very high, squeaky, frightened voice.

"Oh sh.. I've fallen down picking up the box". Jamie heard Zenze mutter words he had not heard before. "My foot hurts, I can't stand on it!" Jamie was panic stricken and in a shrilly voice squeaked "What must I do? What must I do? It's so dark."

"Don't panic!" exclaimed Zenze sternly, the pain making him ultrasensitive. "You now have to think of me and not of you."

"But I am so afraid, cried Jamie, I can't see you and it's so dark."

"Mfana, be calm, for goodness sake I am close to you, snapped Zenze, "take the flame torch and look behind you, I am not far." Jamie holding the flame torch turned on his bottom, he was so terrified he felt his legs were made of jelly. He was not even aware of Xixi's little claws digging into his shoulder. Jamie could just see the outline of a boulder and something like arms waving to and fro,

139

the shadows on the roof looking like tendrils reaching out to him. "I can see you, I can see you!" shouted Jamie, forgetting the 'no shrieking rule', the shouts returning as echoes, 'seeyou', 'seeyou'.

"That's great," muttered Zenze through clenched teeth because the pain was quite bad and he was somewhat irritated by Jamie's fear.

Jamie shuffled on his bottom until he could feel Zenze's hand and then stuck the flame torch into the soft earth as he had seen Zenze do. "Don't panic," repeated Zenze. "But first, did you notice that there is a little bit more light just here? I don't know and no one else seems to know where it comes from, but there is obviously another small opening and the light seeps through." Jamie, looked up wide eyed and realized he was so busy being frightened that he had not noticed he could see a lot better.

Jamie was so relieved he could see a bit better that he made a whoop of joy but unfortunately brushed the torch head onto the damp wall and the light spluttered and died. He held the torch as if in a trance, transfixed and immobile. "Oh Zenze! what have I done?"

Again, Zenze muttered irritably, "that's just great!" but the tone of his voice belied his inner feelings. He was in pain, in a dark cave with a whimpering, blundering young boy. He had to be firm with Jamie, could not show his anxiety or anger, after all it had been an accident. "It's an accident – it can happen. Now is the time to think about what to do next." Zenze tried to stand up, but the pain was too much and he collapsed in a heap. "Eshuwi, eshuwi, the pain is so bad I just cannot walk on my foot, I think I am going to be sick." Jamie, shivering from fear and the cold came up with one of his pearls of wisdom. "I think we are in trouble?"

"We certainly are!", replied Zenze through clenched teeth. "Well, one thing is for sure, I cannot walk out of this cave on my own and I am too heavy for you to drag me, so you, my friend are going to have to go and find help."

"It's so dar.." Jamie started to say, but he stopped himself and said , "Zenze I'll go back to the kraal and get help. Do you think I'll find the way out of the cave? I wasn't really paying much attention when we came in, I was just following you."

"Yes, that is a problem, because there are many passages along the way, and if you take the wrong turn you could be lost forever", Zenze said, emphasizing the 'forever'. The pain was making him a bit mean.

Jamie was breathing quickly from fear. He felt scratching in his pocket and remembered Gerbi and the long cord he had wrapped round his middle. "Of course I can find my way out of the cave, Gerbi will help me." Zenze shook his head in a resigned fashion and rolled his eyes in disbelief, "I know he is a nocturnal animal and can see in the dark, but Jamie, he's a gerbil and has been in your pocket all this time, have you lost your mind? How can he lead you out?"

Jamie told Zenze how at the last moment he had tied the end of the long cord to the bush at the entrance to Gerbi. "All I have to do is follow Gerbi's cord." He felt so relieved that he had found a solution but then he thought of Zenze. "Won't you be afraid to be in the cave on your own with no light?"

"I must admit that I am a little afraid, especially when the bats wake up and go hunting at dusk – you heard what a loud noise they made. I know there are no monsters or dangerous animals in the dark, but"......

"I know! I know!, shouted Jamie, I'll leave Xixi with you, I know how I like to have something furry to snuggle up to. I remember once I had a favorite toy ... I can't believe I am remembering just at this moment, when we are in trouble – he's name was 'favorite' and whenever I felt insecure and especially when I went to bed at night I loved to hug my 'favorite'.

Jamie's mind started thinking in all directions, of all sorts of plans to help Zenze. "I'm going to crawl out the cave with Gerbi, and leave Xixi with you for company. I know you've got water and some food in your bag." Zenze tied the end of the cord that attached him to Jamie around his hand, and propped himself against the wall of the cave moving his head around to try and find a comfortable spot. Zenze was in a lot of pain and kept moaning, "Eshuwi, Eshuwi". Jamie took off his shirt and rolling it up, put it behind Zenze's head. "Better?" he asked "much better," replied Zenze. He was in a lot of pain but, were the pinpricks of tears in his eyes due to pain or pride for this little frightened brother behaving like an adult, all of a sudden making decisions and taking charge?

"I'll keep tugging on the cord and make the mousebird call which you must return until I am out of the cave, then one last tug and you'll know I am on my way," said Jamie. He unwound Xixi from his back and gave him gently to Zenze. "You will look after Xixi, won't you, because he is afraid," he said, with a catch in his throat, scratching Xixi's head, a part of his heart anxious for this beloved pet.

Xixi, in the cave, had become a different monkey. He had become quiet, clingy and needed to be close to Jamie all the time, making only the occasional quiet, tiny 'xi, xi' sounds. Jamie understood Xixi so well. He too sometimes became quiet, especially when he met strangers and found himself in an out of the ordinary place. The loud, cheeky, adventurous Jamie would become, like Xixi quiet and subdued.

"Zenze, I have no idea how long we have been in here, so I think I must hurry away, I don't want to be running back to the kraal in the dark." On an impulse he hugged his brother and said, "see you later." Just those few well known words they had used so often gave them both courage, and Jamie, holding the cord with one hand made his way in the direction of the exit. By feel he had unknotted Gerbi's shorter cord from the long cord, leaving him attached to his usual cord. He knotted a loop with the shorter cord over the long cord so that Gerbi could run unhindered, but was still held firmly by Jamie. His heart beating so loud he thought Zenze could hear it, he crept on all fours as slow as a snail, or so it felt, guided by Gerbi attached to the long cord. Crawling on his hands and knees, he felt the small stones dig into his knees and the palms of his hands, but he didn't mind the pain. The slimy, damp moss made squishy sounds as he slowly moved forward, but he didn't care. His only thought was to get out of the caves.

Gerbi, confused at first, soon started picking up pace and seemed to understand what was expected of him. On two occasions, he must have smelt something that only his gerbil nose would think was interesting and tugged away from the long cord, but Jamie pulled him back on track. Jamie knocked his head on the tunnel roof a few times. He was disorientated and going forward by instinct. He answered Zenze's 'krikk, krikk, krikk' call, then lowered himself onto his tummy and crawled towards the light that he could see at the end of the tunnel. At the exit he gave a last long tug, and a last 'krikk, krikk, krikk call, untied Gerbi, gave him a little kiss on the nose, put him in his pocket and tidied up the bush hiding the entrance to the cave.

Exiting from the darkness of the cave to the outside, for a moment he was surprised by how bright and clear everything looked. He felt as if he were seeing the forest, trees, sky and world for the first time. Everything looked so dazzling, clean and bright. Everything smelt so sweet. Ooh! The smell of that bat guano was just too bad in the cave, Ugh! poor Zenze and Xixi. He took a few long, deep breaths of the clear air and made for the campsite where they had rested the night before.

CHAPTER 15

Help!

amie put Gerbi into his pocket and thought that he could make it back to the kraal before dark if he ran at a steady pace; he didn't have time to waste. He knew Zenze and Xixi would be safer in the cave than in the wild but it was chilly in the cave and Zenze was hurt, so he needed to bring back help as soon as possible.

The sun was still high in the sky, he reckoned he had quite a few daylight hours left before darkness engulfed the forest. He and Zenze had taken a very slow walk to arrive at the caves, stopping for any excuse, kicking of stones, hiding from each other and finding new spoor, all simple things that boys do on an outing together, but now he had to get back as quickly as he could. He grabbed his bag and headed for the path they had taken.

He started running at a slow pace but had to often stoop under overhanging branches or push them aside.

His heart lurched at one point when he heard 'xi,xi,xi' coming from a cluster of trees and he immediately thought of Xixi, who he knew would be afraid and missing him in the dark cave. Turning a sharp corner,  he almost collided with a *badger*, foraging in the undergrowth for insect nests. He stopped for a while to catch his breath and noticed its slow, winding walk while it dug for rodent and reptile holes using its ultra sensitive sense of smell to find scent trails. The badger is one of the most fearless animals in the forest and although small is so courageous that it will take on large poisonous snakes.

At the beginning of this return trip, Jamie felt full of energy and bravery, but as he moved further away from the caves, he realized that he was alone, with only a Gerbil for company, he imagined danger in every shadow and behind every bush. As he neared the stream where he and Zenze had stopped to eat, he again sniffed a whiff of that evil-smelling stink and the hairs on the back of his neck tingled. Could it have been a honey badger? Tiki?"

He stopped for a moment to scoop some water over his head and to sip the deliciously cold water, but what was different? There was no wind, but one tree was quivering and what looked like dollops of pale green and red-striped, gluey muck was falling to the earth.

Jamie could see no animal or bird in the tree, and certainly did not recognize the droppings, he just knew it was something he did not want to meet at the moment, so he ran up the track as fast as he could, continually looking behind him. Why did he feel as if he were always being followed? A pair of red glowing eyes, sparkled in the thick foliage at the top of the tree canopy but Jamie did not see them. Jamie ran through the buff colored elephant grass so tall he could just see over the tops, hoping he would discourage any snakes with his noisy running.

He kept on running until he saw the outline of the trees he was looking for, and headed in that direction. He skirted bushes, full of magnificent flowers, and moving to his left, began hearing the sound of the river. He was on track! He was close to home. As he came over the ridge of a hill, someone shouted, "what's the hurry"? it was Nelson, herding the goats towards their night time enclosure. "Nelson, am I glad to see you, I need your help. I am so tired I cannot run one more step," he gasped. He briefly told him what had happened and asked Nelson to run ahead of him and tell Shaka. He would follow behind him slowly with the goats. Nelson did not hesitate for an instant and started shouting and running towards the kraal.

Jamie sat down for a while, and then walked towards home. By the time he dragged himself towards the goats' corral, most of the village were waiting for him. Children shouted, 'he's here, he's here', the village dogs barked joyously picking up on the children's vibes and high pitched voices. Some children herded the goats for him and he walked towards Shaka's hut, but Refilwe was already running towards him with her arms outstretched, followed by Temba, leading Shaka. "What happened? What happened? How is Zenze?"

Shaka's voice boomed, "let the poor boy get his breath back, bring him something to drink. Come, my son, we need to make plans immediately, you must tell us what to do." Jamie felt so proud and overjoyed that HE was being asked to make decisions. Jamie sat on a log around the fire and started. "Zenze has hurt his foot and needs someone strong to help him out of the cave and bring him home. He has some water and food and Xixi is with him. He hung his head in shame, saying "we need to bring some light as I extinguished the torch by mistake, brushing it against the damp walls". He did not see some of the older boys smile; they had made the same mistake as well, and felt sorry for him. They knew that only through making mistakes does one learn. A few of them gave him a gentle touch on the shoulder and tapped his back.

Nelson said, "I'll go with some of my friends and bring him back – don't worry. Keep a big fire burning to show us the way when we return and we'll be back before the first owl starts hooting," and off they went, carrying blankets and long sticks. Nelson, always the leader, the level headed and practical young man, took control without being asked.

Shaka holding Jamie by the hand, said. "Sit with me, and tell me everything while you drink and eat something." Refilwe and Temba had come to sit cross-legged near them so they too could hear of the adventure. Jamie told them everything that had happened, even how he and Zenze had stopped to have something to eat and seen the bee-eaters and watched the blue cranes fighting over a frog.

He casually mentioned the dreadful odor! Refilwe drew in a quick breath and Shaka's hands began trembling ever so slightly, Temba straightened her shoulders and gave a surreptitious glance into the distance. Jamie gave a nervous chuckle. Then Temba asked, "but how did Zenze hurt his foot?" Jamie jumped up saying in a hushed voice, "the box, the box, Zenze hurt his foot while lifting up the box." In his anxiety to get help for Zenze he had completely forgotten about the box.

"I hope they remember to bring it back."

Shaka remained silent. Temba and Refilwe simultaneously asked, "what box"?

Shaka knew he would have to explain the box to these two women or they would not give him a moment's peace. He knew they would nag and nag until he told them. He also felt that Jamie had to be told how important it was to him. "Well?" asked Refilwe, "why the secret – I want to know." Shaka thought for a moment and said, " Zenze needs to be here when you are told and I think Mfana should rest a while now. No more questions, please, it's late and Mfana needs his rest".

Jamie dragged his feet and collapsed onto his blanket in the hut and fell asleep. While Jamie was recounting his experiences, Gerbi had climbed out of his pocket and Temba fondling him, gave him some seeds, watched him scuttle beside the log lying on the ground, do his toileting, drink water from the little bowl that was always filled outside the hut, wash his face and then run over to the half asleep Jamie. Gerbi tucked himself behind Jamie's neck, in between the blanket, and found a place to snuggle close to Jamie's chest where he could hear his heart beat. He made a few circles, almost as if he were chasing his tail, then settled down to sleep.

During the night, Nelson and his friends carried Zenze back into the kraal where Refilwe made a quick assessment of his injuries. She wrapped his ankle with wild olive leaves as she had done for Jamie, a long time ago, bandaged it, made him sip some muti and reassured him that he would soon feel better. Even though he was a young adult, Zenze did not like taking the muti, and asked whether it was absolutely necessary. Refilwe reminded him how he used to fight and spit it out when he was a baby. How he used to clamp his mouth shut and fight with his parents so as not to take medicine, even though it was for his own good, but in the end he learnt to take it without fuss. Refilwe gave Zenze a sweet date to chew on after the medicine to take away the bitter taste. A lion roared in the distance, a hyena laughed nearby and the hippos foraging on the far side of the river were the last sounds Zenze heard as he finally gave in to sleep.

At the first sound of the cock crowing, Jamie's eyes flew wide open and he jumped out of his blankets. Xixi tumbled to the ground and Jamie's happiness at seeing him made him grin from ear to ear. "Welcome back." Xixi showed him a full set of upper and lower teeth and jumped up and down and then straight into his arms. "Ooh!, you smell of bat guano, later in the morning it is going to be bath time for you." Rolling his blanket and stuffing it in its place he ran out to find out about Zenze.

He ran for about ten steps and then stopped and looked around him. He saw everything in a new light, he was filled with happiness at the familiarity of everything he saw. He loved his home, he felt secure in his family. He laughed at the chickens pecking in the dust for scraps, looked into the trees and with a sigh of relief saw the two loerie birds preening themselves. He gave Xixi's hand an extra squeeze and took Gerbi out of his pocket and scratched him behind his ears.. Even the goats were welcomed with a Jamie bleat, 'maaaaaaaa' and as he passed the pigs enclosure he made 'grunting noises' to which the pigs answered with pig-squeals.

He entered Zenze's hut and as his eyes adjusted to the gloom he anxiously looked towards the heap of blankets. "Don't just stand there, come and give me a hand," said the pile of blankets and Zenze waved a hand in Jamie's direction. "Come and help me sit up I have so much to tell you."

"How are you feeling, how is your leg or foot or whatever is hurting you." asked Jamie.

"Our mother says she thinks it is only a sprained ankle, nothing broken and just a few scratches – I'll survive. Just a few days of rest and I'll be chasing you around the mountains again!" Jamie could not stand still from excitement – he had ants in his pants and so wanted to ask Zenze about the box.

"Did you bring the box back?"

With a glint in his eye Zenze replied "what box?"

"You know, the box, the box."

"Oh, that one" and he teasingly scratched his head pretending to try and remember.

Jamie was beside himself, and with clenched fists he made snake eyes at Zenze, punching the air all around him.

"Yes, of course we did."

"Have you opened it? What is in it, and why the secrecy?"

"Mfana, this is so difficult for me to tell you because……." Just then Shaka, led by Temba and followed by Refilwe knocked on the wall of the hut and they walked into the hut.

CHAPTER 16

...I had forgotten about you...

ou know that blind old men hear far better than you think – what is this I hear about secrets? asked Shaka.

"You are just in time, I was going to tell Jamie about the box."

Zenze did not know where to start, so he just blurted out, "the box belongs to you, Mfana."

"What are you talking about, I have never even seen it?" Is it a present from you to me?"

"No, I found it at the time I found you, it came from the wreckage of the aeroplane." Jamie just stared, as children do when they cannot grasp the meaning of what is being said to them.

"I just don't understand. If it's mine why have you not given it to me before?"

Zenze piped in, "Mfana, I was the only one who knew

about the box until a little while ago. I hid it in the caves the day after we found you. At first I thought about it often, and then somehow it faded into the depths of my memory, just waiting for the right time to tell you. Just recently you have started remembering your language and many happenings from your previous life, so we thought the time would be right to tell you and see what was inside."

"Remember we told you there were bad men who came to look for something at the place where the aero plane crashed? They were not looking for you, they were looking for the box – I overheard them. I was afraid for you. I was afraid that if they found out you were in the aeroplane, they would come looking for you and take you away. You were so badly injured and could not remember anything so, Shaka forbade all the people who live in his kraal to mention that you lived here, just in case they came back for you. We have been waiting to see what would happen and then you crept into our home and hearts and when no one came looking for you, we just kept you with us." Jamie just sat and stared, nodding his head now and again.

"There is something keeping the box locked, so we have to break it to see what is inside. Look what I also found and brought it with me. It was so hidden under all the wreckage that those bad men did not see it. Here it is," and Zenze fished around in his bag and gave Jamie the little red toy. Jamie's legs almost buckled and his arms would not move for a moment and then he held out his cupped hands to Zenze and said, "my little red tractor, my little red tractor, but where is monsieur?"

Temba asked "monsieur – what is that?"

"Monsieur is what I called the little driver of the tractor."

Zenze said, "I suppose that is in your language?"

"Oh no!" laughed Jamie." My parents spoke another language as well and monsieur means 'man.' Jamie cradled the little red tractor, feeling it and turning the wheels, then he put it on the smooth floor, the cow dung floor Refilwe had painstakingly smoothed, and pushed it around and around until they all joined in his joy and laughter, making 'broom, broom' noises with him. "I had completely forgotten about you, little tractor." While Jamie happily pushed his tractor round and round, Zenze had forced the lid of the box open.

"What is this?" asked Zenze as he held up a very scruffy, well used, frayed stuffed animal?"

Jamie lunged at the toy and nuzzled it with tears

running onto it." 'Favi'. 'Favi'. "It's Favourite, Zenze this is Favourite, I told you about him in the caves. He is my best toy in all the world. I remember you!" Nuzzling Favi and then tucking him under his arm, he looked excitedly into the box.

"Hauw!" exclaimed Refilwe, and Temba echoed "hauw". "Mfana, tell us what you see." Jamie, clutching his little red tractor looked in the box. He took out a little box with a lion on it and exclaimed, "matches!". I knew there was an easier way to make fire, I just could not remember. I was not allowed to touch them on my own when I was a baby".

"Magic sticks" murmured Shaka nodding his head.

"What is that bright green 'thing' that looks like a stiff huge caterpillar?"

"Ha, Ha," laughed Jamie, "it's a torch". I wonder what this is?" he said as he held a rolled up map. He was so excited that he did not pay much attention to any one article. He wanted to see them all at once.

"I want to see them all."

He handed the rolled up piece of paper to Temba who unrolled it and turned it this way and that, not understanding any part of it. He saw another smaller box and excitedly opened it. "Medicines, muti," he said.

Refilwe took it from him and handled the small pill boxes, shaking them. "Don't eat them, said Jamie, going to Refilwe, "you must not even taste them, they are good if you are sick, but poisonous if you eat them without knowing what they are for. Children can die if they eat medicines not meant for them. I was taught to never, ever take medicines, unless they were given to me by a grown up person. Sometimes, medicines look like berries or 'sweeties' and children can become very ill if they eat them," warned Jamie.

Refilwe gave him that enquiring look with the big eyes.

"I'll explain 'sweeties' later" he said, "just know that they are delicious to eat."

"What's this?" "Oh, oh, oh, no! – I had forgotten about you! This is my red and white lolette!." No one said anything, they looked with wide eyes, waiting for Jamie to explain. He put this strange object into his mouth and gave a big belly-laugh. Refilwe was dumbfounded. He took Temba by the hands, Favi still tucked in his armpit and did a little dance-jig with her, clamping the lolette in his mouth and laughing so much that a thin stream of dribble escaped from the sides of his mouth, making him sputter and cough. Refilwe, just shook her head

160

and smiled seeing Jamie so happy and so funny with this 'lolette' thing in his mouth. Shaka clapped his hands and chuckled hearing so much laughter. "I remember, I remember this is a 'lolette', I always asked for it when I was tired. Sometimes I called it a dummy."

Refilwe had a flashback to that very first night when he was brought to her. He moaned in his sleep and was so restless, she did what she had done with Zenze, she had put his thumb into his mouth to soothe him, and it had worked! He'd sucked happily on his thumb as many children do, until they are old enough and don't need to any longer. 'This 'lolette' must be something instead of a thumb', she thought. In fact she thought she remembered him muttering 'lolette' as well as 'mommydaddy' in his sleep.'

"What else is there, what else?" shrieked Jamie, in a voice so full of excitement that his words trembled and tumbled into one another. "I wonder what's inside this little pouch?" Opening it, small rocks tumbled out. Refilwe stifled a gasp and said nothing, she remembered the old man who had brought a pouch with similar stones, and she muttered "maaisan." Shaka asked for the stones and rolling them around in his hands muttered, "blood diamonds," while shaking his head.

161

Zenze held a circular object with a moving hand in it. He did not know it, but it was a compass. Jamie, looking over Zenze's hand said, "I really don't know what that is. I suppose it must be important to be in the box. Look, look exclaimed Jamie, "colored pencils and a click pen." Holding the pen up to Temba he clicked the pen. She held the pen and was almost reluctant to click it. "It won't bite, Temba, it is used to write and make pictures. These colored pencils are used to color drawings, but on paper. You know how we draw in the sand with a stick? These are used for drawings on paper." Taking the folded piece of paper he quickly made some squiggly lines on it with the crayons. Temba tried as well and so did Zenze.

"I remember this," exclaimed Jamie, "I was never allowed to hold it – it's a folding knife. " He clamped Favi's ear into his mouth so he could handle the knife. All eyes stared at him as he unfolded small blades, a file and a pair of scissors. "I have never seen anything like that in my life," said Refilwe, "Shaka, you must feel it, but very carefully as it could cut you." Shaka held the knife gingerly and felt the sharp edges with his fingers saying, "this is truly a magic knife that can fold away." Jamie took it back and saw two marks on it – two letters. J.A.

Jamie held up a small magnifying glass to his eye.

"What is that Jamie?", asked Temba. "It's a special glass that makes things look bigger," replied Jamie, while looking at everyone through it. Temba had been fascinated by something bright yellow with spikes on it and could not stop herself from picking it up, only to throw it into the air shouting 'aiee, aiee'. Jamie pounced on it laughing.

"Don't be silly Temba, it is a squishy ball. I love anything soft and spongy, you know that. Oh I am so happy, here catch it", he said, as he threw it back to her.

"There are books and papers and images of people", said Zenze.

"Let me see, let me see." Jamie looked at the photos in the passports with reverence and his hands started to tremble. "I think, I think, I think I know these people and that little boy is ME. Oh mama, are these my parents?" He ran to Refilwe and clinging to her neck sobbed and shuddered uncontrollably.

Shaka put his hand on Jamie's back and realized the time was right to tell Jamie everything they knew. Shaka would have loved to look Jamie in the eyes and tell him everything would be okay, but all he could do was tenderly touch his face, trace the tears and croon to him like a baby. "Tula, tula","shush, shush". Temba just sat and hugged herself, her thoughts a jumble. — Jamie moved towards her, and with big sobs curled onto her lap and held her tightly around the neck, crying quietly.

CHAPTER 17

....only real men are able to cry...

amie rummaged in the box, touching item after item and placing it on the floor with a frown on his face, and then a shriek of recognition followed by a look of puzzled confusion. Refilwe took Shaka by the hand saying they would leave Jamie alone for a while and go and prepare breakfast motioning to Temba to follow them. Xixi touched, licked and tried to taste everything until Jamie closed the lid and took out one item at a time. Xixi sat on the box and banged it with his little fists. It was too early for Gerbi to make an appearance, but he moved about in Jamie's pocket to let him know that his sleep was being interrupted.

After a while, Jamie walked out the hut into the brilliant sunshine and went to sit in the lacy shade of the flame tree where the rest of his family were eating porridge. His shoulders were stooped as if they were heavy, holding Xixi by the hand and kicking any little stone in his path. His mind was buzzing like a beehive. He wanted to ask so many questions, he was remembering songs, words, names, people; he felt as if he were two people. Zenze was drinking from his gourd and said "Mfana, finish your food and then we'll go down to the river to your thinking rock and I will tell you all that I know."

Jamie ate in unusual silence, he was always bubbling with chatter and this silence made his family anxious. Refilwe kept giving him sidelong glances and then letting out huge sighs. The box had brought matters to a head and now was the time to tell him all they knew. Each one of them had something special to tell him.

Zenze moved towards the river and Jamie followed him. Jamie didn't wait for Xixi because he knew, wherever he went- that monkey would find him. He was so alert he knew every movement that Jamie made. Xixi had left the group and gone foraging for food and to play in the trees, jumping from one to the other always avoiding the sharp thorns on the acacia trees. Although early in the morning, the air was hot and thick, in the distance black storm clouds were accumulating with the promise of rain.

Columns of ants scurried to and fro frenetically

moving their eggs to a safer place, a sure sign that rain was imminent. Rain was always welcomed by the village as it meant the crops would grow and there would be plentiful food and water for people and animals. Rainwater was used as drinking water and all the huts had containers for just this purpose. The river water was fine for washing and irrigation, but not for drinking. People living upstream were throwing all sorts of rubbish into the rivers, especially the big factories up North, making the water dirty and polluted. Shaka kept warning his people to not drink the water from the river and to not pollute it themselves.

Zenze lashed the high savannah grass on either side of the path that ran towards the river with his long stick and of course Jamie copied him. Zenze walked silently and a little hunched as if he were carrying the weight of the world on his shoulders. He noticed a snake trail across the path and lashed even harder at that point in the grass. A *spoor* of three forward pointing toes and one toe angled backward told Zenze that a flock of *guinea fowl* had walked across the path, probably on the lookout for snails, ticks or berries. He knew they weren't far as he could hear their call 'keet-keet' 'keet-keet'. He pointed to the spoor and imagined them quietly picking their way through the undergrowth. Had they been alarmed their cry would have been 'chik-chil-chrr.' Zenze looked at Jamie, who acknowledge him with a nod and a smile but his gaze was clouded and his mind was still racing with many questions, he felt as if he were in a whirlpool.

As they approached the river, the sound of running water had a soothing effect on Jamie as this was his very special spot, a place he often visited when he needed to think and be quiet. They walked along the river, moving long branches out of their way, their footsteps more labored as the mud stuck to the soles of their feet. Jamie's special rock was an outcrop of rocks jutting half out the water. The only way to reach them without wading into the river was by climbing a tree with a huge overhanging branch that reached the dry part of the rocks.

Zenze stopped in his tracks, just before the tree and pointed into the mud – hippo 'imvubu', he said.

The spoor, four toes, each with a heavy broad nail on the fore and hind feet was quite fresh and damp. He stood very still, so did Jamie. They looked intently into the reeds on the riverbank for any sign of the barrel shaped animal (see page 198). Not only did they look, but they listened as well because the hippo is not the quietest animal and makes a lot of noise while walking through the reeds. Jamie said "They are all in the river, I can see their eyes, nose and ears on the surface of the water."

"You are right, we are safe, let's climb the tree."

Zenze crossed the thick branch first and Jamie followed, arms outstretched helping him balance. Usually, Jamie would have showed off for Zenze, balancing on one foot, or pretending to lose his balance, but today he walked across the branch steadily and with purpose. He was nearly pushed off by Xixi who was following them and jumped onto Jamie's shoulders. Instead of laughing and pretending to be surprised, Jamie just held the little paws that were on his shoulders and felt something prickling in his eyes. Surely he was not going to cry? Oh well! if he was going to cry, then he was going to cry. Shaka had once told him that only true men were able to cry because it took a courageous man to cry.

Settling on the rock in the dappled shade of the leaves from the overhanging branch, Zenze began his story. He repeated most of the story Jamie knew, adding the finding of the little red tractor, and how he had overheard the men looking for "a box". How he had found the box quite by chance and hidden it first in the baobab tree and then the caves. How he had saved Jamie from the hyenas.

I'm so glad I didn't end up as hyena food!" said Jamie while sniffing loudly.

"When we found you, Mfana, we thought you were about 4 years old but we could not understand you. In your confusion, when your fever was very high, you kept on asking for 'mommydaddy' and 'lolette' but no one knew what you were saying."

"There were people who worked in the town who could have helped with the language but we wanted to keep you a secret for fear that the bad men would come and find you. You had a great bump on your head because you could not remember anything. You were very injured so Refilwe kept giving you muti to make you sleep. You slept for a long time, occasionally waking up to be fed and changed, until you were well enough to walk around. Temba, Refilwe, Shaka, Nelson, Kabo and I slowly, slowly taught you our language and until recently we thought you had forgotten all about your previous life and language. Now you are beginning to remember not only your language but also people and happenings."

In a trembling voice, Jamie asked, "those men, who

were they? and what were they looking for?"

"They must have been looking for this box, and now, I think they were looking for the diamonds in that pouch. Somehow your parents were involved. As to who they were, I just don't know.

"All I know, Mfana, is that it looked like they took two bundles that looked like people, or bodies with them, and I think they were your parents."

"But why did my parents not come back and fetch me?"

Zenze had dreaded this moment for so many years and rehearsed all kinds of answers but all he could do now was keep trying to swallow the big knot he felt in his throat. "Mfana I don't know what to tell you other than how I saw it – it looked like they put two bodies on the back of the truck. I don't know whether they were alive or dead but I did see a little bit of golden hair sticking out from under a blanket.

"My mom?"

"I don't know, I don't know"

"My dad?"

Zenze just shook his head and lifted his shoulders in the universal shoulder shrug that says 'I don't know'.

Jamie felt so sad that, holding his knees, he pressed

his head down hard and sobbed uncontrollably. Zenze crept next to him and put a hand on his shoulder, while big tears like a silent waterfall slid silently down his face. After what seemed like ages, while the hippos dived and made splashing noises, butterflies and dragonflies flitted from one reed to the other and the eternal miggies niggled around them, Jamie unfurled himself, wiping his nose with his fingers. Xixi had gone to look for berries, Gerbi crept out of Jamie's pocket and on impulse, climbed to his neck and began licking his salty tears, trying for a reaction from him. Jamie heard and felt nothing, he was so distraught. Ants were walking over his feet, dragonflies flew past them and a blue *kingfisher* made a few swooping flyovers and daring dives to catch a fish with its large red bill for its lunch, but Jamie saw nothing. He didn't even hear Zenze telling him that kingfishers ate insects as well as fish.

Sniffing and wiping his nose on his arm, Jamie whispered "I don't know what to do".

"You don't have to do anything at this moment. Mother and father want to talk to you when we get back, maybe they have a plan. Mfana, you have been with us for such a long time that we do not see you as being different to us. At first, we were afraid of the bad men coming back for you, but we also always hoped that someone of your family would come looking for you. Then as you grew older, we asked people in the big town if anyone was looking for a young white child and no one seemed to be asking about you. You have become so part of our family that we stopped seeing you were different to us. But, Eeish! just look at the color of your skin and eyes and your hair that is almost white and you must agree that we are more handsome than you!" This last was said in a light hearted manner, just to try and break the seriousness of the moment. Jamie felt a little better as they walked towards Shaka's hut.

CHAPTER 18

....the belt that Temba wore all the time...

efilwe met them under the Flame tree where she was stirring a huge pot of stew over a blazing fire. "Your father has gone into the forest to talk to the ancestors and then to his old mother and won't be back for a while, perhaps she will have some wise words for us. She is nearly 100 yrs old – can you imagine that?"

"Mfana, I have been slipping back in time, thinking of so many things and wondering whether we should have spoken up sooner, but only now that we have found the box, have certain events become clearer, also, you are now old enough to understand, whereas before now you were still a little boy." Jamie felt pleased in being told he was no longer a little boy.

"Quite a while after you came to us, one night an old man was found wandering aimlessly by two goatherds. He had been travelling for a long time and was looking for Shaka's kraal, because he had an important message for Shaka. However, the old man, ill and disoriented was not able to give a full account of his message. He spoke in a language not quite like ours, but Shaka and I were able to understand that he had come from far away, from a kraal that had a secret entrance and was guarded by warriors, wild animals and strange creatures. He had managed to leave the kraal with the help of a lady who had given him a pouch with stones. She was a special, golden haired lady who helped the sick. She had two different colored eyes, one was the color of grass and the other of the sky."

Jamie shivered, he remembered looking into those eyes. Refilwe continued. "She was a medicine lady, and they respected her because she cured their illnesses. She helped the children to be born and gave the women advice on how to look after them. The old man made a sign crossing his wrists, showing that this lady had been brought to the kraal with her wrists bound. He would often find her looking into the distance and shedding tears. She was loved by the women, but especially by one of the Chief's son's wives who goes by the name of Ntsepe." At this point Refilwe dropped her eyes, hugged herself and a lonely tear ran down her cheeks, "Ntsepe, my niece," she whispered. Temba instinctively touched the beaded belt around her waist and whispered "mama?" Refilwe nodded her head.

"The old man said that he helped the medicine lady find the special plants, herbs, seeds, pods and grasses she needed to make muti. She, was not allowed out of the kraal but, he was trusted and allowed to roam the forest and hills at his leisure, outside the kraal, looking for the special plants. One day, after the old man had not been feeling well for some time, she told him that he would soon die because she did not have the muti to make him well. She had been so kind to him that he wanted to do something for her before he died, and that was why he had come looking for Shaka's kraal."

"The lady had said that just before the flying silver bird went down, her husband had pointed out Shaka's kraal and how beautifully located it was, in the bend of a river, almost an island. Because he often left the kraal to go looking for the ingredients for her muti and stayed away for days on end she assured him that, when he was missed, she would tell the Chief and his family he had not returned from outside the kraal, and only the worst could be expected. The secret would be theirs and theirs alone. She was not sure that Shaka's kraal was the right place for him to go to, but it was a hunch she had and it was her only chance to get a message out."

"She gave the old man a pouch with a symbol on it that she had drawn with black dye. From the weight of the pouch he could feel they were stones but there was something else he did not recognize. He described how she had held him close and in a choked voice said, 'maaisan,' and then moved away before anyone could see them"

"The old man," continued Refilwe "whose name was Amagogo said he had been travelling for so long that he had become disoriented and could not tell us exactly from what direction he had come. Shaka and I gave him some hot broth, wrapped him in a blanket and left him to sleep next to the fire saying, "tomorrow you can tell us the rest of your story". A frivolous wind picked up some stray leaves and tossed them onto Refilwe as she walked away. "Uffa!" she exclaimed, "where did you come from, wind?"

The wind crept up her skirt and lifted it, so that she had to turn around to straighten her skirt and, as she did, a rotten smell drifted past her and for the briefest of moments she saw a pair of red eyes in the darkness. "How strange" she said aloud to Shaka "for a wild animal to bring its hunt so close to us humans" Shaka stood absolutely still and said "that is not the smell of a kill, that is the smell of something bad – think happy thoughts and it will go away." He bent down and took a fistful of dry earth, throwing it over his right shoulder saying "you will not harm my family or anyone of my tribe – be gone evil spirit."

The next morning, as the sun's rays were painting the sky in ever changing hues and the cocks started crowing, Refilwe gently shook Amagogo awake but she could see that he was very ill. An owl gave its last hoot of the night and the two loeries shrieked 'goway goway'. At Refilwe's gentle insistence he stirred and said "maaisan", closed his eyes and left this world, clutching the pouch.

A curious *gecko* stared with unblinking eyes from the roof of the hut at the spider that was unwittingly walking on its web towards a trapped fly – little did it know it would soon be the gecko's breakfast.

"My son, I have known deep down that there was a connection between my niece and this old man and I now think there is a connection to you as well. You said "this is **MY** father and this is **MY** mother, when you looked at the photos, you spoke in your language and that word 'my' sounds like part of 'maaisan'. We think it means 'MY son."

"Of course, of course" cried Jamie, "my dad always called me 'my son' and so did my mom, at times, she also called me 'my superstar.' The pouch, have you still got the pouch – what is in it?"

Refilwe dug deep into her pocket and took out the pouch and handed it to Jamie. He was so impatient it took him a while to loosen the knot and pulling so hard on the cord, the stones fell out and with it a lolette (dummy) this one a yellow one with tractors on it. "Oh yes! this must be from my mom, it is my lolette. She must be alive – I know she is alive – she must be alive," muttered Jamie. "The stones are the same as the ones in the box!"

Everyone was quiet, thinking their own thoughts. The sounds of Shaka's footsteps intruded in the silence partnered by the steady steps of Temba leading the old chief towards them. "I feel such heavy thoughts in the air, let me sit down as I have news for you." We need to clear our minds and think of what we are going to do. So much has happened in such a short time that I need to take one fact at a time and talk about it with everyone so that we can make decisions."

He sat on a rounded rock and began. "Refilwe and I

promised Ntsepe that we would look after Temba and try to make them meet sometime. Ntsepe was very sad and unhappy to be Wakiri's son's wife, but we had to obey Chief Wakiri's wishes. She left us without looking back, her spirit broken because she had to leave Temba behind. Now again, Wakiri is making demands on us. This time wanting Temba for his nephew Drako," turning towards where he knew Zenze was sitting he stroked his chin and said, "and I know there is someone who really does not like Drako!" Zenze shifted uncomfortably and clenched his fists. "We feel that now is the time for Temba to go and visit her mother and ask for help. Temba should be allowed to marry Ami whom she loves and who loves her – not someone who does not know and love her. Times are changing and we need to change with them. Mfana, you coming into our lives has brought yet another side to the story."

"Refilwe and I think that Ntsepe and Jamie's mother are in the same village. It is an odd coincidence, yet all the facts point to that end."

"But how, but where, but....."interrupted Jamie.

"Patience child, I don't know all the answers now either. Let's all say what is in our hearts and then maybe we'll come to some decision. Jamie, staring into the distance asked, "how long ago did this old man visit the kraal?" Refilwe answered "I would say it was about 5 years ago." I remember as it was soon after Shaka lost his eyesight."

"I want to go to my mother but how will we know how to get there?" said Temba.

Shaka continued, "as you know, I went to visit my old mother and she told me something very interesting and exciting. While Ntsepe was preparing for her marriage, she spent much time with her grandmother sewing clothes and beading belts, pouches, necklaces and bracelets – all part of her dowry, gifts to bring with her to her new home. Something she never told any of us was that she overheard some of the warriors, who accompanied Horrifendi to our village, talking about the journey they had just undertaken and were discussing the journey back to take Ntsepe to her new home. She told her grandmother all the details and together they beaded a special belt with all the information. It is the belt that Temba wears all the time.

"My mother is old and cannot remember all the details but let's see what the beads say. Temba, take off the belt and let me feel it. Is there a black edge to the belt with two red beads here and there? She said the black edge that surrounds the belt is a dark place inhabited by the Evil one. The two red beads here and there in the edge are its eyes. She thinks one of the yellow patches is the desert sand where nothing flowers except for a few weeks of the year. Is there a yellow patch with flowers"?

"Yes, yes" said Temba with a trembling voice, full of emotion.

"I've seen such a place. It is a place of magic," said Shaka.

Old Gogo (grandmother) said that the blue beads that wind through the belt show the river that has to be crossed, and the occasional green and brown beads sewn together show crocodiles and hippos in the river."

Again Temba said, "yes, yes. I have looked at that belt so often and wondered about the patterns."

"Look" said Refilwe, "that strange tree that looks like an upside down tree with roots in the air must be a baobab tree. They are trees that house the spirits of our ancestors. Some are so huge that twenty people holding hands could not surround its trunk. Animals, insects and other plants all live in those trees. In fact that big, furry, green seed that you boys kick around is a baobab seed. The tree where Zenze hid you on the night he found you, Mfana, was a baobab tree – do you remember?"

Shaka said "this part about the baobab trees was important but old *Gogo* cannot remember why. Temba pointed and said "look she has beaded an elephant and a giraffe. I can see rhino and buffalo as well. I think the brown beads in the trees could be monkeys."

"I wonder what the white and deep pink beads in this blue piece are?" whispered Refilwe.

Shaka answered, "those are the flamingo birds in the big lake. I know where that lake is – it is far away. Does the belt show something that could be a waterhole?"

"Yes," said Temba with a quivering voice "the elephant and giraffe are beaded in a patch of blue, with grey, black and various colored beads in and around it – I think it could be animals and birds at a waterhole."

Shaka said. "I well remember that waterhole. Many animals and birds visit it. I remember seeing birds I could not even name. It was a long time ago, but I can head you in the right direction."

"Old Gogo remembers a big rock with red spurting out of its top as something Ntsepe heard the warriors talking about. They spoke about its shadow. Are there some black beads showing a shadow? It was important, something about the shadow at sunset. They called it the mountain that bellows and shouts and spews fire." Jamie squinted close to the belt observing. "She has beaded a horse with a rider but look at the rider, it looks like he has a cloth across his eyes, I wonder why he is blindfolded?"

"Mfana, the warriors were saying that no one is allowed to go through the entrance with open eyes. The entrance is a closely kept secret. Horrifendi does not allow strangers into the village. That old man gave up his life to give us this message. The warriors said that they were afraid of the journey back because there were many dangers along the way and one of them joked and said they were lucky that the horses knew the way!"

Temba hugged herself as she thought of all the love and foresight her mother had had. She thought of all the long hours she must have spent beading and imagined her with tears dripping onto the belt, thinking of the little girl she had to leave behind. Temba touched the belt and held it to her cheek, then she inhaled deeply trying to smell the tiniest hint of her mother. Her aunt, Refilwe, had been like a mother to her, but in the deepest part of her being she so longed to hug her real mother again. She had to find her, she was sure she would help her to not have to marry Drako.

CHAPTER 19

....how I'd like to see those sights again.

haka held onto his walking stick and said, "I was once a young boy, like you, Zenze, when my father told me that I was to attend Initiation school or as you call it 'making-of-a-man school'. I was terrified but too proud to show it or to tell anyone. It was part of our tradition and in those days, we thought it would have been a bad omen on our family if I had not attended. But, that was many years ago and times are changing. I too am changing my ideas. I am going to tell you all a story that will help us for the future decisions and choices we are going to take."

"Four other young boys and myself were taken out of our huts in the middle of the night, stripped of our clothes, blindfolded and marched into the forest. We were terrified and fell often, only to be hauled back onto our feet. We knew we were about to begin our initiation but it was always a shock as it was so sudden and unannounced - we had been dreading it for months. No one knows who the men are who come to take you but they are vile smelling and cruel. Today I do not see the need for cruelty but in those times, ideas were different. I do not believe that cruelty teaches anything, but kindness and example are the true teachers.

We walked through the forest, over streams and through land I barely recognized. At dawn we stopped. By this time our legs and feet were bloodied as we had fallen often and bumped into branches and stones. My blindfold had loosened a little and while we rested and ate some dried meat, I peeked to see where we were. I worked out the direction we had come from by looking at the position of the sun. We were soon on the move again and I kept a memory in my mind of where we were. At noon, we rested again and this time our blindfolds were taken off as our 'guides' felt we would be so disoriented that we could not possibly know our whereabouts".

"We stopped at a river where the mud is a particular red color. We were told to smear our bodies with the mud mixed with some animal fat. Eish! did we smell! The men wore loincloths but the rest of their bodies were painted with mud in different colors, especially white that made them look like ghosts. They had also painted their gums and teeth red, by chewing on the bark of a tree, so to young boys like us they looked very fierce indeed!"

Our little group huddled together, all thoughts of being brave faded. We were terrified. I am telling you this because I want you to know that it is, as Jamie would say 'okay' to admit that you are afraid. While blindfolded I took note of the ground we walked on, listened to the birds, animal sounds and felt the shrubs and trees around us. I had a reasonable idea in what direction we were headed and when at last we could see, I knew exactly where we were.

While you were explaining Temba's belt, I realized I was familiar with many of the clues. I have been to the great lake where the beautiful pink and white birds with bright pink legs live. I saw them lift up into the air like a huge cloud, flapping their wings, making a loud noise and seeing the wonder of the black underside of their wings.

They are *Flamingo* birds. I am happy knowing that you will see them too."

"You can imagine how terrified we were when we

encountered the big beasts of the plains, with nothing more than a small spear. We were taught how to track, how to keep downwind, how to survive on the wild berries and the odd wild rabbit we speared. At times even the poor geckos provided us with a small meal. We were always hungry – you know how young boys are always hungry."

"One night, while we huddled together for warmth and courage, we were woken by the earth trembling, the trees shaking and the usually silent day-time birds shrieking. Our guides laughed and said it was a wicked demon that had come to eat us as we were so useless and valueless and the ground trembling was its footsteps. The nocturnal small animals ran around in circles and in strange ways. We saw a monkey run up and down a branch tearing at its fur. We saw a snake fall out of a tree and scuttle backwards from fear. No! I never want to go through that terror again. Just as we thought the worst was over, there was a loud bang and a bright light shot up from the top of the mountain closest to us."

"We clung to each other and then a fine grey mist settled on our skins and the most awful smell, like rotten eggs, covered us. It was so bad I had to be sick in the bushes. We looked like grey body-less ghosts with only two black holes for our eyes. It wasn't a demon, it was a volcano. What is a volcano? It is a mountain that has a very hot centre and when the inside of the mountain becomes too hot, it bursts from the hole on the top. Just like burning wood sometimes makes a loud popping noise and sparks shoot from it, or when water boils out of a pot. What the volcano spews out of the top of its head is very, very hot stones and melted sand that looks like a river and burns everything in its path. It was a very, very frightening experience, but full of magic and one that I can never forget. I think the guides knew the volcano would erupt and they enjoyed seeing our terror. I think that is the mountain in Temba's belt."

"You tell me there are two yellow patches and I think I know what they could be. Further away from us is a strange land. Just as we live in a forest with many trees, streams and good, rich soil to grow our crops in – there are other places in this country that are very different. We came across a land that is eerie in its starkness. (Namaqualand). The guides told us it was a desert and that it seldom rained there. Only at a certain time of the year, it rains and then the whole world is transformed from a desert into a place of wonder. We saw plants that live nowhere else in the world. Plants that looked half dead and aloe trees with strange shapes like scarecrows standing in an empty field. In particular a plant they called a 'north watcher,' a tall plant with fine hairs on its trunk with the uncanny habit of always turning its head to the north."

"What really shocked us when we returned through this spot on our way back home was that we could not recognize it! Something magical had happened. It had rained. Wherever you looked it was a riot of colors, pink, yellow and orange. We were so excited that even though we were still hurting from our initiation we lay down in the flowers, rolling on our tummies, looking at the bees and the insects diving from flower to flower. We were wild with excitement and called to each other at every new plant or flower we found. Fat green fingers poked out of the hot sand as if they were holding bright pink flowers. Grey wormy looking tendrils reached for the sky and then coiled back to the ground like a curly sheep's head. In between some stones I found a bright red tiny plant of the reddest of hues – a bloody red. I still remember it."

"The mountains, Eish!, the mountains. When you see them, be my eyes because they are so beautiful I don't have the words to describe them. All I can tell you is that you are aware of their presence at all times and look carefully because they change hue as you look at them. They are at times brown, then purple, then dark red with streaks of white etching them. They surely must be the home of gods – they are so beautiful. Sigh! We had seen no animal life on our first trip through this desert but on our return trip we saw the odd ground squirrel scratching under a leaf and faint rustling showed a mouse scuttling away. A shadow on the ground and we looked up to see eagles gliding with the hot air thermals."

"The other strip of yellow with a blue band – that can only be beach and sea. This country has the most beautiful stretches of beach sand and sea. The sea is so vast and blue, with seagulls diving into the foam of the waves for fish. Big and small fish live in the water the likes of which we will never know. The noise of the waves is deafening and can be a little frightening. The sand, oh! the sand. It is fine and white with seashells edging the sand like an embroidery." A small hand clutched Shaka's shawl and tugged at it.

Jamie interrupted Shaka with a trembling voice, "I remember, I remember going to the beach with my parents. I remember digging in the soft sand and running to the edge of the water to splash in the waves. I remember being happy but being a little afraid of the sound of the waves. I remember big rocks jutting out of the water with shells sticking to them and rock pools with crabs and tiny fish in them. I remember my mom showing me the different kinds of grasses that grew in the water . I think she called them sea weeds." Jamie was breathless as he said this, and had a faraway look in his eyes. Shaka tapped him on the head, turning his sightless eyes on this little boy that he loved so much. He so wanted to protect him from all sorrow and hurt, but he knew that he couldn't, as Jamie had to face his future on his own.

"Yes, Mfana, you must have been there, because one can never forget how surprised one is at the sheer size of the sea. There is water as far as the eye can see with a line on the horizon where it meets the sky. When the sun sets over the sea, it seems as if the sun throws a stretch of sunrays over the surface of the sea, then slowly disappears behind the horizon line like a great big ball of fire.. Oh! How I wish I could see that sight again," sighed Shaka.

My children, I think it is time for you to go on a journey of discovery. Temba you need to visit your mother and ask her whatever you want to know. You are of an age when she must help you decide about your future. Zenze, it is the right time for you to visit Wakiri's kraal to pay your

respects and ask
about   initiation.
And Jamie, it is time for
you to find out about your parents."

Jamie jumped up like a bolt of lightning, smacking his legs and waving his arms about. He was so enthralled with Shaka's story that he had not noticed a line of *ants* crawling up his legs.

CHAPTER 20

....he saw a figure walking towards him...

amie walked through the opening of his hut with mist swirling around the huts giving the impression that they were floating and moving. The smell of smoke particular to kraals was even more pungent in the thick air and he had a feeling that a new life was beginning for him, almost mystical. He scanned the area around him not really looking for anything in particular because he knew every nook and cranny of his kraal.

He walked towards the embers that had glowered all night and stoked them with a stick, blowing gently on the cinders to start a flame. He heard before he saw a figure walking towards him, eerily silhouetted in the mist. "I hope it is you, Zenze and not a ghost approaching me," chuckled Jamie. "I need all the help from a full-blooded warrior on this journey, not some scary, eerie person. Zenze hunched down and warmed his hands holding them in front of him towards the fire.

"I don't know about you, but one part of me is excited to go on this journey and the other part of me is a bit afraid," said Zenze.

"That is exactly how I feel and you know, when I am afraid I start to fidget and talk too much" replied Jamie. Zenze gave a smile that dazzled in his ebony face but he said nothing. They both turned to face the shuffling sounds and knew that is was Shaka accompanied by Refilwe. "So eager to start your trip?" remarked Refilwe.

Shaka felt for his sitting log and held out his hands to the fire as well. "Good morning father"

"Saobona, my sons." The goats started bleating in a frenzied manner and Shaka remarked, "Nelson must be saying goodbye to them, or maybe it's the other way around. We all know what a good goatherd he is." Just then Nelson and Temba appeared, and they too gathered around the fire.

"Well," said Refilwe, "as soon as you have eaten your porridge you can be on your way. I don't have to tell you that I love you all and will be waiting with open arms for your return. Heed the wise words of your father and make sure you have everything you need for your journey. Nelson, we will expect you back first. As soon as you have found the entrance to Wakiri's kraal, turn around and come back to us to let us know that our children are safe." Refilwe, like all mothers and grandmothers, had difficulty saying goodbye. She wanted to say so many encouraging words and words of love but when the time came to actually say goodbye, the words stuck in her throat and she was silent, mouth twisting and trembling to stop the tears she knew would follow All she did was put a leather thong with a bead around each child's neck, squeeze them in an embrace and mouth "I love you."

It was a motley group that left Shaka's kraal, each with their own private thoughts. The last sight Refilwe had of them was their outline against the horizon with the sun, a big orange fiery ball, peeping above the ridge; a tall teenager with a gangly walk; a girl on the edge of womanhood; a smaller boy holding a long stick and a young boy with hair glowing like fire holding hands with a monkey, and a gerbil on his shoulder. They had discussed the direction they were to take and they headed towards the rising sun with a spring in their step.

They walked in single file, full of excitement. At first they were familiar with their surroundings, but then they veered to the left and found themselves in unknown territory. Temba checked for the umpteenth time that she had the belt secured around her waist. Jamie checked that the cord around Gerbi was secure and put him in his pocket. Xixi's jumped onto his shoulder, "You are going to have to get off my shoulder soon Xixi as you are becoming heavier by the day" chuckled Jamie. You cannot want to 'uppies' all the time."

"Uppies?" what is that Jamie?" asked Temba who was close on his heels.

"When I was little I used to want to be carried all the time, and I used to say 'uppies time' but my parents said I had to walk a little longer as it would help my muscles grow strong I cannot believe I am remembering so much.

They moved slowly, everyone deep in thought. Would they be able to find the hidden kraal? Would Ntsepe remember Temba? What and who would Jamie find? Zenze led the group with Nelson in the rear. They left the protected area of the kraal and moved towards the forest that surrounded the village. They were moving downwards and Jamie turned to take a last look at his home, noticing the swirling smoke from the fires and the figures of Refilwe and Shaka silhouetted against an orange dawn. His stomach muscles constricted and a lump formed in his throat, as he lifted a hand in a farewell gesture. His breath caught in his chest as he noticed the smoke swirls interlinking and a shape, looking very much like a monster, sending tendrils out towards them. He didn't say anything, he touched the bead around his neck and turned to watch where he was going. They kept on moving downwards towards a part of the river that was dangerous and fast-moving. They heard the river and Zenze said "we are nearing a place where there are many hippo, so be aware.

See, this is a hippo pathway, look at the spoor. The reeds have been trampled. The hippo always use the same pathways and we would be very unlucky if we did not move away should they be heading this way."

They walked a little longer and from a vantage point a little higher than the river bank, Jamie gasped in awe. He had seen a few hippo near his home, but never had he seen so many of all sizes together. Some were just lying on the sandy river bank, some were rolling in the sand, those in the river were wallowing and occasionally pushing each other as they touched. Some *hippo* were trading threatening gestures, opening their mouths wide in a yawn and making guttural sounds These enormous creatures always fascinated Jamie, especially when they were submerged in the water with only eyes, nose and ears above water.

"Look" said Temba, there's a baby hippo peeking from under his mother's belly. Zenze, who was standing nearby said, "don't think the hippo is just a big fat lazy beast that wallows in the water all day doing nothing. He can walk on the bottom of the river and by doing so it moves the sand, opening channels for the river to flow. A curious fact about hippos is that when they dive, their ears and nostrils close automatically. They don't have to hold their nose like you do Jamie, when you dive." Jamie gave him one of his looks and grinned.

They moved along the river, always keeping well above the water line and as they rounded a bend, Nelson, leading, lifted his hand and said *"buffalo"*. On the opposite side of the river, stood a herd of buffalo. Some were moving towards the water, some already drinking and

some were shunting each other out of the way to roll in the mud. There was almost a feeling of playfulness in the herd, they seemed very relaxed. Some young buffalo bulls paired off and sparred in mock contest, knocking their low slung horns together. Nelson pointed to the buffalo on the fringe of the herd that were sniffing the wind for signs of danger. "The buffalo has very poor eyesight and has to rely on his sense of smell to tell them of impending danger, those on the fringe of the herd are the lookouts."

Temba pointed and said "look at how many birds that buffalo has on him. He must have very many ticks sucking his blood. There are even birds eating the ticks from its mouth and ears."

"Those birds are not only keeping the buffalo clean, but they are scouts as well, warning the buffalo should there be danger nearby," added Nelson.

They walked a while longer and then stopped to eat under the shade of a toon tree. While munching on some dry mopani worms and biltong they became aware of the sense of calm and vast open space so typical of the African savannah around them. It was not yet the rainy season and the veld looked dry-yellow and brown with the occasional smattering of washed out green thorn trees. The air tasted dusty. Midday in the African bush and nothing stirred – the world was taking a siesta from the heat. As Jamie drifted off to sleep in the shade, a particularly strong dust devil whirled itself around him, causing Xixi to chatter in fright, jump down from the tree he was sitting in and curl into Jamie's back with his hands around his neck. Gerbi snuggled deeper into Jamie's pocket. The wind ripped the water calabash from its moorings in a tree and broke Jamie's spear. The water from the calabash poured green into the red earth and smoke tendrils crept into the still air giving off an odd smell.

Temba shook Jamie awake. "It's time to start walking again". Jamie looked at his calabash, creasing his forehead in a frown. He picked it up and realizing it was empty, mentioned it to Zenze who took it to fill it with his own one. "What is this sticky, green gung? Yuck! Jamie, where have you been keeping this poor calabash?"

"Honestly, Zenze, I left it hanging from a branch of that tree, full of water, and when I woke up I found it empty on the ground." Nelson had walked towards them and with one swift action threw the calabash into the thick bush while saying, "drag your hands through the dust, rub your hands well then let me pour fresh clean water over them. I don't like what I am hearing and seeing. This broken spear, I don't like it. Something strange is in the air, let's move along."

Jamie started shaking ever so slightly, thinking 'could it be Tiki?' Temba put her arms around Jamie, giving him a hug and led him towards a path that vanished into a tangle of vegetation, thick with vines hanging from the upper branches and a deep carpet of groundcover and thorn bushes. Xixi immediately started swinging from vine to vine as if he were the leader of the pack.

"I'm confused, Temba, muttered Jamie," looking over his shoulder.

"So am I, little brother. There are some things that I just don't know. All we can go by is our instinct. I too felt the evil that Nelson felt. He is far wiser than us, put your trust in him."

"Do you think it has anything to do with those red eyes your mother beaded into the belt?" asked Jamie in a hushed voice. Temba just shrugged her shoulders.

They walked silently, concentrating on the path. The forest grew denser and thus darker. Thick ferns grew abundantly, their long fronds curling from the centre forming a soft lace–like turf as far as the eye could see. The odd African orchid peeped its red head through the ferns' soft, filigree-like foliage, catching the uneven rays of sun that filtered through this canopy of leaves, a strange mound of dead leaves hiding a mushroom.

All of a sudden they were in a clearing, where they could see signs of a long- dead fire in the centre. Zenze held up his hand and whispered," there is a *korhaan* bird close by. That whistling call is a male's call. We are going to see something spectacular."

A korhaan usually spends most of its time on the ground, well-hidden among the low vegetation, but becomes a real show-off when he spots a potential bride. "There he is! He is such a dull-looking bird, mottled brown with long dark green legs, but what a character!"

They heard a loud clacking of its bill, a high rising, whistle-like call, 'chew, chew, chew'. It ran a short distance before taking off vertically, flying straight up almost past the umbrella of tree tops, folded its wings and legs and then plunged down, tumbling over and over, its plumage fluffing out, its russet colored crest on display, opening his wings at the last moment to glide elegantly to a resting spot.

Jamie was transfixed, Temba covered her mouth with her hands. Zenze and Nelson had big grins plastered on

203

their faces, they were so pleased to have seen this rare sight, certainly one of the most magnificent sights of the African bush.

"I almost cannot believe what I have just seen – what an amazing way for a bird to try to catch another bird's attention," said Jamie and with that he spread his arms like wings and proceeded to circle Temba making a whistling sound like the korhaan, 'chew, chew, chew'. Nelson and Zenze joined him while Temba made shooing sounds and pretended to try and run away, only making it worse because they chased her even more. After much laughing and whistling they all collapsed in a heap and caught their breath, Xixi had become so excited chasing the children that Jamie had to hold him close to calm him down. Gerbi must have felt confused with all the jogging he received in Jamie's pocket.

That knotty feeling in the pit of his stomach niggled at Jamie as he lay down to sleep that night. What lay in store for him? Could his mom really still be alive? Why had she not come to fetch him? Would he recognize her? Would she still love him? Maybe she was dead and not at the kraal? What about his dad?

CHAPTER 21

....the seeds come out with its pooh...

he umbrella of foliage thinned out and the sun began filtering through the canopy warming their bodies. They had been walking uphill steadily and as they stepped into the brilliant sunlight they all shielded their eyes with their hands. The landscape before them was in stark contrast compared to the dense forest they had just left. Before them appeared a barren scene with trees standing like skeletons in the dust, all trampled and warped. "Elephant," said Nelson, "they have been here and broken most of the trees. The elephants usually eat the leaves to the height that their trunk can reach, but in dry times, they push over trees to get to the fresher leaves at the top. These higher-growing leaves are the giraffe's food, because of course they have a much longer neck. What happens is that new shoots grow from the foot of the trees, and this becomes food for the shorter

animals like zebras, wildebeest and many other grazing animals. By eating the seeds the elephant helps more trees to grow."

"I know how the seeds are seeded again, they go through the elephant's stomach and come out with its pooh," chuckled Jamie.

"We call it dung," said Temba, with a stern face that made Jamie laugh even louder – being a boy he was fascinated by all forms of dung. "Because elephant travel vast distances in search of food, they spread the seeds far away. The dung fertilizes the grasslands and dung beetles and termites break up the droppings and take them below ground where it feeds the roots of plants."

"I would never have known that." said Jamie, "I hope we can see a dung beetle pushing a big ball of pooh with its hind legs." He gave a sidelong glance at Temba, to see whether she would correct him using the word pooh, but she chose to ignore him.

"It's been a while since the elephant were here, lets cross this bare patch quickly," said Zenze. Jamie took Xixi by the hand and moved towards a row of baobab trees silhouetted on the skyline. The ground underfoot changed slowly from hot, parched earth with the only sound the sound of feet trampling dry, broken branches, to sparsely grassed tracks. They could clearly see a well-trodden path and no one said anything but it was certainly an animal track, especially one used by elephant because of the broken upper branches of the trees. The dung they could see was not very fresh, meaning the elephant had passed this way a while ago, so they moved with ease.

The little group was happy to be out of the hot sun and stopped in the shade of a huge baobab tree, leaning against its trunk and looking up, and touching its majestic trunk. No matter how many times one sees a baobab tree, the sight is always breathtaking by its sheer size. "Could this be the baobab tree shown on Ntsepe's beaded belt?," wondered Temba aloud.

"Maybe," said Zenze "we have come in the right direction. I see people have stopped here. I can see they rode horses and made a fire. It's probably a good place for us to rest the night."

Nelson set about making a fire and rigged three sticks from which hung a black pot half-filled with water. Temba swept the area around the fire with a branch to make it clear of insects, especially the deadly scorpions, while Zenze and Jamie moved around looking for dry sticks for the fire because it had to be kept alive all night. Xixi was already swinging from branch to branch in the baobab,

upsetting a *hornbill* pecking termites on
the bark –giving off its 'kok, kok,kok,kok'
call.   Jamie held onto Gerbi's cord while
he ran along low lying branches in the
surrounding lower trees.

   High up in the tree, the trilling call of
the barbet aggressively defending its nest could
be heard – 'trrrrr, trrrrr, trrrrr'. They all regrouped
to sit around the fire waiting for the porridge to cook.
Jamie, lying on his back looking at the sky through the
tangled branches of the tree asked no one in particular
"tell me about the baobab tree," and Zenze started.

   "I need not tell you that it is the largest tree in the
forest, you can see for yourself. It is home to so many
animals and birds. We have just seen the damage that
elephant cause, especially on the acacia tree but just
turn around and look at that baobab with strips of its
bark hanging down. That is the work of elephant. They
particularly like its bark, but once the bark is stripped off
a tree, insects and disease attack its inside and the tree
eventually dies."

   "What a shame" said Jamie sadly, while scratching
Xixi behind the ears, Gerbi at his feet eating some seeds.
The African night arrives quickly with a spectacular pink-

orange sky. The calls of the birds in the trees that had reached a crescendo of feeding frenzy and twittering just a while ago, slowly, slowly quieted down and only the odd rustling or irritated squawk to protect a chosen perch could be heard. The two loeries jostled for a comfortable perch, making enough noise for Zenze to look up and shake his head. A hot mantle of darkness descended with only the stars and the fire for light. The night was so clear that it seemed as if the stars were near enough to touch. Nelson stoked the fire, stirred the pot with a stick and with a sigh sat cross-legged near the fire. "I hope we'll see elephant tomorrow, Mfana, I love those big beasts. Once I went hunting for food with my father and we came across a herd of elephant and he told me so much about them. Did you know that it is the old mother cow elephant who is the leader of the herd? When young bulls reach a certain age she nudges them out of the herd?"

"Ha!" said Jamie, "that means that Zenze, Nelson and I, would be nudged out of the kraal when we are a little older?"

"Oh! What a glorious thought," piped in Temba. "I would be rid of you three and then maybe I could become the leader of the village?" This kind of bantering always caused a reaction, usually laughter, and even this time the hot, dusty, wild bush reverberated with four young voices laughing and making howling calls to the moon.

Jamie pretended to kick Zenze who made a mock elephant charge towards him, his arm extended from his nose like a trunk. Nelson, flapped his hands close to his ears making a trumpeting sound. Temba picked up one of her skirts and shooed them away from the fire, doing the occasional dance twirl, dance steps handed down from generation to generation of women. Totally at ease with the moment. A young girl on the brink of womanhood. The three boys, after much whooping and counter dance steps one by one came back towards Temba poking fun at her by bowing to her and asking her forgiveness, teasing her by saying, "forgive us Great Lady Chief." She giggled touching each on the head.

They ate, then curled round the fire for the night. Nelson immediately fell asleep. Zenze felt that uneasiness that usually happens just before sleep. What lay ahead for them? Temba could still hear the laughter in her mind and wondered for how long she would be part of it. The thought of losing this unfettered freedom; of the responsibilities of being an adult and married to someone she did not love was too much for her, and she choked back a sob, then she too fell asleep. Jamie fondled the bead attached to the necklace tied around his neck. In his other life, he remembered touching his favorite fluffy toy to help him sleep, and now Favi was back with him in his box. Xixi curled into Jamie's back while Gerbi lay in his pocket. Would he find answers at the end of the journey? Would Temba have to leave their home? Sleep came easily and he dreamt of riding on someone's shoulders and thinking how wonderful it felt to be so high in the air, looking down at a golden lady holding her arms out to him.

All of a sudden the fire crackled angrily, sparks flew into the air spraying the sleeping children with purple, orange and yellow specks, but they were asleep and no one saw anything; not the pair of red eyes, not the hissing sound nor the angry tail that swished in the baobab tree – only Xixi heard the drip, drip of something fetid falling to the ground and clung even tighter to Jamie and then his eyes closed as well.

CHAPTER 22

....I have never seen anything like this in my life...

elson stoked the fire, Temba gathered her sleeping blanket, giving it a good shake, Zenze shook Jamie and said, "wake up, Mfana we need to make an early start and I want to look at that belt again."

The orange sun peeped above the purple grey mountains and at the moment when night and day meet, when the world is so quiet that all noises, even the very faint ones can be heard, when all is grey and misted, it seemed to Jamie that he was no longer sure what was real and what was not. It took him a few seconds to make out where he was, and what he was doing in this strange place. As the stars disappeared, the sky was replaced with a resplendent canvas of pinkish-orange splashes of color, interlaced with a brilliant blue African sky.

Temba untied the belt gently and gave it to Zenze who held it one way and then the other. "I think we should be coming to a large water-hole, which is what our father thought. This part here in the belt, with a large blue circle looks like it could be a water hole. The grey, brown and black beads around it that might mean animals. I think we are on the right track".

"Zenze," said Jamie, "I was so excited to be coming on this journey, but now, this morning I am feeling a little unsure."

"You are not alone in feeling unsure, both Temba and I feel that way. She is very afraid of what we are going to find, at the end of our journey. None of us knows. We must keep in mind why we are going on this journey. We are looking for answers." Nelson handed them both a cut out calabash with watery porridge, touching each one playfully on the head and the three boys drank in silence. Xixi ate the remnants of Jamie's porridge and Gerbi licked from Zenze's calabash. Temba sat on a log a little way away deep in thought.

They cleared the campsite, making extra sure to douse the fire by throwing sand on it and chose a barely visible path to start the next leg of their journey. Yet again there was a surprise in store for them. They climbed higher and higher, leg and calf muscles screaming from pain. As they reached the ridge of the top of the mountain, they were greeted by a carpet of red. The entire mountainside was filled with aloes of every size each one in flower with long red clusters looking like red-hot pokers. "Wow," exclaimed Jamie, "I have never seen anything like this in my life before." Xixi ran towards the nearest aloe and felt it and then ran quickly back to Jamie. Temba stared in wonder.

Zenze asked "is there anywhere on the belt that shows this?

"I don't think so," said Jamie, "perhaps the plants were not in flower when the guides spoke about it."

"Clever boy, you might be right," piped in Nelson, "I don't see a path so we are going to have to make our own one. Be careful of those sharp points, especially for your eyes. I know that the watery inside of the leaves is a good medicine for scratches, but it would not fix an eye. Listen to the buzzing of the bees, they are having a field day sucking up the nectar from the flowers. Shaka once told me something quite strange, he said that without bees pollinating our crops and fruit trees, nothing would grow. Imagine that?"

They walked in a single file, calling out precautions to each other. "Watch out for the slippery stones," or, "watch out for the pointy leaves, be careful of the bees." The slope downwards was quite steep and the sand underfoot slippery with pebbles. At one point Temba's pride was hurt when she lost her footing and did a head-over-heels, landing ungraciously on her back, fortunately only her pride and nothing else was injured. No one laughed or teased her, only too aware that she could have hurt herself badly.

From the vantage point of the hill, they could see that further down the valley there were more and more well-trodden paths and at one stage saw a herd of soft-fawn and white *springbok* walking delicately and elegantly in one direction some stopping to graze. "I think those springbok are heading for a water-hole," said Zenze. All of a sudden the Springbok started 'pronking' as if to give the children a show. It is one of the most graceful sights in the animal world, where the springbok do a ballet-like routine in which they literally seem to spring up into the air, legs held ramrod-stiff, heads lowered, back arched, hairs on their white rump fluffed out. "Every buck," observed Nelson, "has its own markings and peculiarities. All springbok have that white underbelly and a thick stripe running from back leg to foreleg and a white bottom."

"I am getting excited, said Zenze "I think we are going to see many animals at the waterhole. It is early in the morning and many will come for their first drink of the day." As they rounded the corner of a hill, below them they saw the waterhole. "Let's find a place in the shade where we can watch the waterhole without being seen. Jamie check the direction of the wind, " it should be blowing towards us and away from aimals." Remember to move slowly and not make any quick movements. Animals always look back to see if they are being followed, always on the alert for danger coming from behind."

A few dead trees peeped out of the surface of the water, many birds perching on its branches. The outside of the hole was well trodden and in places sandy while in others muddy. It is a strange fact but the different animal species do not fight for the water. There is an understanding that when their thirst is satisfied, the herd moves along leaving a space for the next animal.

"I have always loved the zebras," said Temba, "they are

my favorite animal, so neat and 'well dressed'. Zenze looked at Temba with a smile in his eyes. "You are such a girl, you love to dress up and you even dress-up the zebras."

"I like the way the black and white stripes are slightly different on each zebra, no two zebra are the same. I must say they have the shape of a donkey but with stripes – they are truly one of a kind," said Temba. The zebra drank their fill and then moved on, the foals touching noses with their mothers, it's the way Zebras keep in touch with each other.

The *giraffe* moved forward to drink and Jamie and Nelson waited for the moment when, because of their long legs, the giraffe splay their front legs and then stretch their long necks to drink the water. Nelson nudged Jamie and they both grinned. After quenching their thirst the giraffe moved a little way away and started munching the tender top leaves of some nearby trees. "Of course, they always eat the sweetest leaves at the top of the tree because no other animal can reach them; no other animal has such a long neck," said Zenze. Within a few moments, the giraffe had moved deeper into the dense bush and only their heads with small horns could be seen. Giraffe are masters of camouflage, able to stand perfectly still and together with their dappled coats, they blend into the background. One moment you see them and the next they are gone. "It's amazing," said Zenze " they are so big and tall and yet they can disappear in a moment. Did you notice that some of the giraffe had little tufts of hair growing on their horns? Those are the females."

Nelson nudged Jamie with his elbow and whispered, "I have been waiting a long time to see this animal – look a *rhino*." Jamie's heart stopped – he had never seen one but had heard people speak with awe of this animal. There he was, a rhino standing on the opposite ridge. It moved forward towards the water, his characteristic gait of heavy head close to the ground. Jamie sucked in air and stared at this huge animal with a large horn on its nose and a smaller horn a little way back towards its small eyes. "It's a white rhino," whispered Zenze, "it has a square mouth and hump behind his thick neck." The rhino lumbered heavily towards the water on its stumpy legs, drank its fill, at ease with all the animals around him. A short way away a mud pool, soggy and squishy looked very attractive to the rhino, it casually walked towards it, rolled its enormous body in the mud, snorted, shook itself and slowly walked away.

"Zenze, you said he is a white rhino but he looks grey."

"All rhino are grey, but there is a difference between the black and white ones. Black rhino have a different shaped mouth; they have a hooked lip and eat bushes more than grasses. Can you believe there are wicked people who kill the poor rhino for its horn?" whispered Zenze.

"Whatever for?" asked Jamie.

"They are so stupid, they think the horn will give them more power and be more of a man."

"How could anyone kill such an amazing animal. Surely if you have to kill something to make yourself more powerful you are less of a man?"

"I agree Mfana. What wise words, I think you are growing up." and with that he gave him a playful punch on the arm.

Gerbi felt uncomfortable in Jamie's pocket and scratched to get out. Jamie shifted position and helped him out of his pocket onto the grass while tying the cord to his wrist. The loeries that tracked them, flying from tree to tree, from the moment they left the kraal, started making a loud noise in the trees above their heads. Jamie frowned, the lines on his forehead etched between his brows. "Where's Xixi? He felt his insides quiver. He had been concentrating so hard on watching the animals that he had forgotten about Xixi who was never far from him. Immediately Temba and the boys looked around on the ground and then up in the trees.

"I haven't seen or heard his gibbering for some time" said Zenze. Jamie made his clicking call-sound, but there was no rustling or answering 'xi, xi'. Jamie had noticed a troupe of monkeys on the far side of the waterhole, frolicking on a tree and a dead log, some even splashing in the water – a lookout on the log on the alert for the crocodiles. Now squinting his eyes he tried to see whether Xixi had gone to make friends. "Is he with those monkeys?" he asked no one in particular. All eyes turned towards the troupe. "I'm not sure, but there seems to be some scuffling just behind that log and I wouldn't be surprised if it was Xixi making mischief. Yes, yes it's Xixi showing off - what a clown," laughed Jamie.

"Oh dear! I see trouble," said Zenze, pointing to a spot in the water. A crocodile, eyes just popping above the surface of the water, headed for a spot, quite close to the monkeys, hidden from the outlook monkey by shallow reeds. It reached the water's edge, short stumpy legs pulling its lengthy body, tail swaying to and fro stopping to look at the monkeys' antics. It was too close to Xixi for comfort.

"Oh no! oh no! cried," Jamie, that silly monkey is showing off so much, that he is not looking out for danger and that crocodile has him in his sights. The monkey outlook started jumping up and down, waving its arms and shrieking, alerting the troupe of danger, but Xixi carried on being silly, doing cartwheels and rolling over and over in the sand. The monkey troupe scattered but Xixi still carried on jumping and rushing around.

Without hesitation, Jamie jumped up and ran down the embankment towards the riverbank shouting, "Xixi, Xixi". Nelson lunged at Jamie to stop him running, but missed him. Jamie picked up some small stones on the bank of the waterhole and started throwing them at the crocodile, but the reptile kept on moving silently towards Xixi. Jamie took aim and threw a stone in Xixi's direction and this caught the monkey's attention. Instinct took over and he immediately ran for cover up a tree. Zenze shouted "Mfana, come back immediately, look what's coming this way." Zenze was angry with Jamie. "That was a very silly thing to do. You put yourself into unnecessary danger, there could be hidden crocodiles waiting for a dim-witted boy like you on the bank. Not only did you endanger yourself, but us too. What were you thinking?"

Jamie stuttered ....."but Xixi, he, he".

"Don't 'but Xixi' me, you did something dangerous and without thinking and I am very angry with you!" The children felt sorry for Jamie that he was getting a tongue lashing from Zenze, but they knew Zenze was right.

Temba cut the tension by saying, "amazing! they were not there a moment ago." Through a cloud of dust a huge

elephant, covered in mud, looking like a ghost, appeared through the thick bushes followed by her herd. Ears flapping, she headed straight for the crocodile. The crocodile stood its ground but the lead elephant, with a couple of nudges of its trunk and foot made it quite clear that the crocodile was not welcome and it reluctantly slid into the water, tail thrashing the water.

Jamie closed his eyes against the scorching yellow of the sun, inhaled loudly and sighed. That monkey is really a monkey thought Jamie. As if reading his mind, Temba cleared her throat and quietly said, "don't worry Mfana, he's safe". Jamie looked back to where Xixi had been and was relieved to see him high up in a tree, looking back at them as if to say, ' see, I'm okay.'

The group stared at the elephant herd, not believing their luck at seeing so many elephant. Babies stayed safely between their mothers legs, peering timidly at the world around them. One old matriarch remained on the ridge as a lookout while the rest of the herd took their fill of water. They used their trunks to siphon water into their mouths and sprayed themselves to cool down. The children watched as with great tenderness some of the elephant fondled each other with their trunks, the little hairs on the trunk helping with their sense of touch.

"I am just amazed that even though they are so very, very big they are so gentle," said Jamie. "See how that mother is spraying water into the mouth of her baby with such care".

A few elephant walked towards a muddy spot, eager to have a mud bath.

"Eish! this is such a treat. What do you think Gerbi, do you want to join them for a mud bath to get rid of those little lice that live in your fur?" asked Jamie jokingly, as he placed Gerbi on his shoulder. Do you know, Gerbi, that Xixi might have been eaten by a crocodile? I'm still shaking inside, I don't know what I would do if I lost either of you."

Two elephant lay down in the mud while squirting themselves with mud and water with their trunks, then stood up and sprayed the babies who followed them. One baby must have been a newborn because it had no idea how to use its trunk. It was quite comical to see the baby try to use its ungainly trunk. In fact it takes quite some time for the baby elephant to learn its many uses. Elephant take mud baths not only to keep their skins free of parasites but also to cool down. Elephant are so clever, they use another way to keep cool, they flap their ears using them as a fan.

A series of rumbles and squeaks could be faintly heard; it was obviously a way of communicating in 'elephant talk'. Only when an elephant senses danger or makes a charge does it make his very awe inspiring trumpet call, while flapping its ears. It is so frightening that you would never forget it if you ever experienced it.

"I know you told me those two white tusks are actually two overgrown teeth, Zenze", said Jamie, trying to make friends with him again. "Do they ever lose their tusks"?

"Yes, they might break a tusk, but the broken tooth keeps growing throughout its life," replied Zenze in a tone of voice that implied he was still furious with Jamie.

A wild rustling in the tree above their heads and Jamie just knew it was Xixi . "Come here you furry, bad monkey. You gave me such a fright, scolded Jamie as he hugged Xixi. Please, please, please don't ever stray that far from me again."

Xixi picked up Gerbi and started grooming him, separating his fur and then picking out a flea and eating it. Xixi, happy to be back with his family, after a narrow escape, was enjoying the attention.

The morning was almost gone. It was time for them to leave the waterhole. Jamie was having such a good time he was reluctant to leave. "Please let's stay a while longer, I haven't seen so many animals before," said Jamie looking at Nelson pleadingly, who showed his palms and shrugged his shoulders.

"We can stay a little longer. In fact I am enjoying watching these animals as well. I love them. I so worry about their future. I hate the fact that hunters and poachers and also farmers kill some of them instead of learning to live peacefully with each other. I wonder whether my children and their children will see them as free as they are now," said Nelson.

The afternoon was wearing on and the children were feeling overwhelmed by all that they had seen. A falcon flew to its nest with a lizard in its beak for its little ones. They were all concentrating on the birds in and around the water's edge, when suddenly Nelson whispered *"Lion"* and they all dropped to their stomachs – they had secretly been hoping for this. From out of a clump of buff colored veld-grass appeared the majestic head of a male lion, resplendent with a thick mane of fur around his neck. His well-muscled body rippling with strength and power, he ambled towards the water's edge with an air of dignity, his movements a fluid dance. He lapped at the water, tail swishing to and fro and soon a bevy of females with their cubs followed. One went close to him while the others held back, waiting for him to finish dinking, then shyly moved to the water and drank their fill. The lion moved away and lay down under the shade of a tree, his huge head not moving much, his well-forward eyes gazing into the distance.

The lionesses paid no attention to the cubs, but kept an eye on the water for the crocodiles. The cubs, some very young, their fur still mottled, cautiously drank the water then, just like human babies, began exploring. Cubs are very inquisitive and began frolicking in the shallows, chasing each other then moving a bit further up the bank stalking and tumbling over each other, the skin on their bodies moving with their movements – they had a lot of growing into their skins to do.

The children could not see too much detail from where they were watching, but two of the cubs must have found a lizard or bug and were stalking it, playfully touching it with their large paws, throwing it in the air, then rolling over, wrestling, while one ambushed its mother as she walked towards the shade. The lioness gently made as if to give him a gentle flick of her paw, made a particular rumbling sound in her throat which probably said "leave me alone now," and the cub moved to another game. One by one the pride of lion moved towards the shade where the male lay, and rested, the cubs still playing and exploring. "We are so lucky to see lion, said Zenze, because lion do not need to drink every day. They can go a few days without drinking. We might have missed them."

"Look, look." Here come the most organized hunters in the wild. I know them well," said Nelson, "I have trouble with them attacking my goats when I am in the hills. I call them *'ixhwili' wild dogs*. A wild dog is about the same size as a medium sized dog with a body covered in a patchwork of black, yellow and white colors. Its rounded ears are large and its tail white-tipped and bushy. The tail is used as sign language. The leader 'talks' to the rest of the pack by moving the position of his tail. If he wants them to turn right he moves his tail to the right. When he is tired, he drops his tail to between his legs and the next wIld dog takes the lead. They are very sociable animals, always moving and hunting as a pack.

"You look worried Nelson," said Zenze, "what is the matter?"

"Just seeing those wild dogs has made me think of my goats – I hope Kabo and his friend are looking after them properly. Once a wild dog has decided on his prey he and the pack will chase it until it is so exhausted it can no longer run any further. My goats have no chance against a pack of wild dogs."

Reluctantly with many backward glances, Jamie and his friends left the waterhole. Nelson felt it would be too dangerous to remain as many animals moved around the area at night and he didn't want them to find themselves in an unsafe place. He had noticed many *lion paw-prints*.

"Temba" said Zenze, "I want to see that belt again. We are on the right track, I want to make sure we are moving in the right direction."

CHAPTER 23

....I feel as if we are being watched...

The group moved through muddy patches interspersed with sand as thin as powder. Broken branches and huge elephant dung pats showed that elephant had passed this way quite recently. Jamie started walking backwards on all fours, saying "what am I, what am I?"

Nelson played along saying "you are a funny boy walking backwards like a dog on all fours, unfortunately you do not have a tail."

"I think you are a cat digging a hole before doing its business," said Temba.

"Come on, Mfana," laughed Nelson, "we know you are pretending to be a *dung beetle*. I know you cannot resist watching those beetles – the minute I saw that elephant dung I thought to myself, Jamie is going to look for a dung beetle rolling a ball of dung with its back legs."

"I am puzzled as to how they can roll a dung-ball so much bigger than themselves for quite a distance, then bury it and lay their eggs in it. Imagine being a dung beetle baby and hatching in dung, eating it for food. Ugh!", exclaimed Jamie.

"Move along, move along," said Zenze, "we have a long way to go and we don't know what lies ahead of us. Let's not forget why we are on this journey."

Late afternoon sunlight filtered through a grove of acacia trees, a film of red dust hanging above the ground creating a mystical, orange-yellow background to the black silhouetted trees. Ant and termite hills dotted here and there gave the impression of hugh incisor teeth sticking out of the earth.

They decided to camp there under the trees where the ground had been swept clean and no grass grew. Others had been there before them. Immediately, each one made themselves useful in their own way. Nelson started looking for sticks and twigs making loud noises and stamping the ground to frighten any animal hiding in the surrounding grasses; Zenze walked around the perimeter swinging a stick this way and that to discourage any unwelcome snake, while looking into the trees;

Temba fussed with the blankets, pots and food holders. Jamie helped look for sticks but as usual was waylaid by insects, birds or whatever caught his fancy. Xixi, a very important part of getting to know a new camping ground swung from branch to branch, alerting the children to any danger.

No one said anything but the site had a 'mystical feeling' about it. As the sun dipped quickly, the sky became a brassy color with the heat of the day seeping through the hard-packed red earth. They ate, for once in relative silence. In the quietness, the bush rustled with the sound of nocturnal creatures hunting for food, or just afraid or inquisitive of these strangers in their territory.

In the distance they heard the lonely cough of a lion and the manic 'whoop' of the hyena. Temba cradled Gerbi, her thoughts far away. Would her mother remember her? How would she feel about her? Would she be young looking or old?

An unnatural light diffused itself around them and Temba hugged Gerbi closer to her asking, in a shaky voice. "What is it? What is that light? Are they ghosts?" The dark clearing transformed into a magical, brilliant, bright ball. Nelson made some scary 'ooooooooooh,' 'ooooooooooh' sounds and said, "Temba don't be afraid, they are fireflies. They are beetles and I'll have you know that the male beetle is the one that is shining the brightest, the female's glow is weak."

"I know, I know" replied Temba, a little irritably, "in the animal world the male species is stronger and more beautiful." It was unusual for Temba to react so irritably but she had immediately thought of spirits, and this worried her, because she had felt a spiritual presence since they arrived, but could not identify it. Why was she so sensitive?

Sleep did not come easily for the children. They tossed and turned and were aware of every little stone under their blankets. Jamie dreamt again of the lady with the golden hair, he wanted to touch her but she kept disappearing.

Against the black night, the four sleeping bundles, drenched in moonlight, did not hear the sinister, distinct hiss that floated over them like a black, undulating blanket. A purply-black mist enveloped them, the foul smell making them cough in their sleep. As two red pinpricks moved in a circle around them, leaves started to wilt immediately.

Zenze woke everyone up very early the next morning. He'd doused the fire, cleared camp and urged them all to get up and get going, telling them they could stop to eat a little later in the morning. Xixi, nose to the ground loped around trying to interpret the sinister disturbing smells he was picking up off the ground. To Xixi they were alive and powerful, but to Jamie, Xixi's behavior was strange. Xixi tugged on Jamie's hand and pulled him away from the clearing, Gerbi peeking out of Jamie's pocket nibbling a seed, stopped munching, sniffed the air and retreated into the depths of Jamie's pocket. The two loeries that had followed them every step of the way shrieked 'goway' 'goway' flying from branch to branch away from the clearing.

As they left the clearing, Temba glanced back, her natural graceful walk a little stiff, showing a tenseness and a need to hurry away. She had noticed the wilted and seared leaves. They moved into thick bush. "Are you sure this is the right path?" asked Temba.

"No", replied Zenze, "I am going by the sun. This seemed to be the only track I could find leading from the clearing. I looked at the belt again and it seems we need to move towards a stream."

"Zenze, don't tease me, if I tell you something, but I feel as if we are being watched. I have been uneasy since last night," said Temba quietly. He put his arm around her and whispered in her ear, "I have had the same feeling for quite a while, so keep your eyes and ears peeled and if you see anything strange touch your ear to let me know". The track led them through densely growing acacia tees. They slipped and held onto branches down a steep hill towards a stream they could hear rushing over stones. Wading through the stream, Temba washed some of the thorn scratches on her arms and Jamie complained that the thorns had attacked him as if they did not want him to go any further. Gerbi had a drink of water and Xixi, as usual, splashed and waded in the shallows but he was nervous, something was worrying him, he kept twisting his head from side to side, making 'xixi' sounds.

They walked through a thickly wooded ravine and turning the corner of the hill, were assailed with an awe inspiring sight. As far as the eye could see extended a vast, desolate plain of dry scrubland, the odd termite hill sticking out of the ground and thousands of thorn bushes, dotted here and there.

Zenze nodded his head and pointed to a gigantic outcrop of sandstone rocks, packed together in a higgledy-piggledy pattern. Some boulders looked as if they were about to fall at any moment.

A cloud of dust on the far horizon and a noise like

thunder made Zenze stop and listen, holding his hand up for everyone to stop. He squinted into the distance and said, '*wildebeest*,' luckily they are moving away from us. It looks like a large herd galloping, something must have disturbed them, maybe lion. I can make out their white tails and horns that point forwards and upwards. Some tribes call them 'white tailed gnu,' because of the whistling sound they make when upset."

They all looked with awe as they neared this stony hill. Something about it made them feel a measure of mystery and anticipation. As they reached the large mound, each in turn touched the stones reverently and Xixi even licked them. A steady trickle of pure spring water flowed from the deepest inner centre of the heap of stones into a shallow pond, which was really just a dent in a large stone. "This water is delicious and cool," said Temba cupping her hands to catch the dazzling water. Jamie cupped his one hand and with the other introduced Gerbi to the water. "Drink my furry friend, this water comes from way down in the earth and is as pure as you can find." Gerbi took little sips and washed his face. Zenze remarked, "this is definitely that brown patch on Ntsepe's belt. Shaka said this site is used as part of the initiation ceremonies. That's why he knew about it." Zenze clenched his fists and ground his teeth, he was so tense at the thought.

"He said to look for scratches on the stones showing animals and other drawings, also to wet the drawings to see them better." As they climbed higher among the rocks, they saw the engravings. Elephant, zebra, gemsbok and ostriches. An engraving of a lion with a human handprint at the end of its tail intrigued them. "Now I am sure we are on the right path. Shaka said the hand at the end of the lion's tail showed a mixture of human and animal features and he believed spirits had the ability to change in this manner. He said it was a link between the present and the past. He said witchdoctors and shamans were also able to do so."

"Do you believe that?" Jamie asked his friends.

"There are certain happenings in our culture, that cannot be explained," replied Temba, while rubbing the goose pimples on her arms, remembering the green liquid that squelched out of Jamie's water calabash and the wilting leaves.

Jamie shrugged his shoulders and moved away from the group and as usual poked around in the rocks with

Xixi encouraging him. He stopped in his exploring and stared at something with a piercing look. It was a scratch in a rock showing a stick figure with a skirt. "Come and see this, I think I have found something. This drawing is the same drawing as that on the pouch that the old man brought to the kraal, I noticed it when Refilwe showed me the pouch. The scraping does not seem as old as the others, it is very clear." His voice had an excited high pitch to it and his heart was thumping like a drum. "Do you think my mother could have carved this? Do you think she stopped at this place and scratched the surface to leave a clue?" Jamie was breathless, the others stared and at that precise moment a loud rumbling noise overhead made them look up, one of the boulders had dislodged and was tumbling towards them.

"Run everyone, run!" shouted Zenze and shrieking with fright, Temba grabbed Jamie's hand and in the nick of time moved out of the path of the huge stone. Temba looked at Zenze and touched her ear in their secret message language and Zenze nodded.

With enormous eyes and shivering from head to toe, Jamie said "It is just not possible that that big stone could have come down on its own. We are the only people or animal here," his breath coming in big gulps. He pulled

Temba down to him and whispered in her ear, "do you think it's Tiki?"

"I don't know, I just don't know" she whispered, her eyes wide with fright, the whites of her eyes luminous against her beautiful ebony-colored skin.

Zenze said "I want to get away from this place. I am afraid and I cannot explain why it happened. Temba and I have both been edgy for some time, but we haven't said anything because we didn't want to frighten you. We feel as if we are being followed. We think there is something or someone that does not want us to find Wakiri's kraal, that wants to frighten us or lead us in the wrong direction. That last clearing we stayed in and this site are obviously sacred places, places that our ancestors visited for special occasions. I certainly am not going to be frightened away, although that boulder nearly crushing us has really shaken me."

They clambered down the rocks on legs wobbly with fear. Temba went straight for the bubbling fountain, to fill her gourd with water but let out an enormous girlish shriek, "aai, aai, aai." A thick green, slimy slush had replaced the pure liquid and a foul smelling mist rose from the rocks surrounding it. She felt like gagging. Picking up her skirt she trembled and squirmed, turned her back to the rocks and started walking hurriedly away.

"Yuck"! said Jamie, "what's going on? Wait for me Temba, how do you know what direction to take?"

"I don't care where I am headed, I just need to get away from this scary place."

Zenze and Nelson joined them pointing to a spiral of smoke in the distance. "We must head towards that smoke rising from that mountain."

"The volcano Ntsepe beaded into her belt?" asked Jamie.

"Absolutely," voiced Nelson.

They moved quickly through the thorn bushes, Temba hugging her skirts to her, but still some thorns managed to snag her clothes. With an annoyed gesture she tugged at them but would not look back, so afraid was she. "Stop it you nasty thorns, you are not going to hold me back. I am going to find my mother. Leave my clothes alone!" Red dust from the earth curled around their feet and made Jamie sneeze. The rainy season had not started and all around them the earth was arid and dry. But, why were there so many dust spirals when the air was as still as still as could be? Why was the dust so fine it crept into the children's mouths, ears and nostrils causing them to cough and splutter? The dust stung their eyes making them water and the more they rubbed them the itchier they became.

Jamie, coughing and spluttering, with Nelson bringing up the rear battled to breathe. Temba, ramrod stiff walked holding her nose. Zenze muttered those angry words that Jamie did not understand. At one stage a dust devil turned Jamie right around so that he faced backwards. Xixi clinging to Jamie's neck made retching noises. The children felt a fear that was almost palpable, and then, just as suddenly all was back to normal. They looked at each other in awe. Had they imagined it?

CHAPTER 24

....he had lost his voice

 head of them a vast expanse of greenery spread itself along the horizon. As if drawn by a magnet, Xixi let go of Jamie's neck and ran towards the green trees. "Be careful Xixi, don't go too far, wait for us," shouted Jamie, but it seemed that Xixi had misplaced his ears and pretended not to hear. He scuttled away, straight as an arrow.

A long, hot while later, as if a line had been drawn in the earth, the vegetation changed to green, lush, thick trees, vines and ferns. They heard a rumbling sound, at first only a whisper, a hum, then as they moved through the undergrowth, pushing aside the vines hampering their progress, the sound grew louder. "It's raining and that sounds like thunder," said Jamie. Droplets of water, catching the sun's rays, looked like a cascade of diamonds dripping from the trees and ferns. Temba gazed in wonder at a spider's web, translucent against the misty background. Their footfalls were quiet against the thick layer of dead, moist leaves. No one said a word. The contrast between the dry, barren land they had just walked through to this lush, cool, moist forest was so extreme it was eerie. The children had entered a rain forest caused by water sprayed into the air by a waterfall.

"That's not thunder and this is not rain," said Zenze. "We must be near a big waterfall."

"I wonder where that naughty monkey has got to" said Jamie "since that episode with the crocodile, I realize he does not know how to live in the wild on his own. He is not as aware of danger as he should be."

As they walked deeper into the rain forest the foliage grew denser and they became wetter and soggier, continually wiping their wet faces in order to be able to see where they were walking. They were unsteady on their feet, slipping and sliding here and there and much to Temba's embarrassment she again slid on the dead leaves and landed with a thud on her bottom. Jamie immediately ran to help her to her feet and he too slipped and landed across Temba's tummy, splattering her with mud and debris. There was no laughter and both stumbled to their feet while Nelson and Zenze looked the other way pretending to be very interested in something in the distance. Only their shoulders shaking and their refusal to look at the two messy, mud splattered friends gave a clue that they were having a good laugh at their expense. Gerbi, a little frightened and possibly a little flattened by the fall, crept out of Jamie's pocket and shook his little body until his fur stood on end.

Temba furious, shook her skirt and stamped her feet. She used the edge of her skirt to wipe her face, glaring at Jamie who just shook his head and said "girls! – I was only trying to help."

Zenze hissed "Shhhhh" holding his finger to his mouth. He pointed upwards into the canopy of trees and whispered "*leopard* in a tree with a dead mon..." and his voice trailed into nothing. He could not believe his eyes. "Nobody move." The children tried to locate the leopard but in the dim light of the forest it was difficult to see it, the rosette-shaped spots on his body blending with the dappled weak light filtering through the trees. Its camouflage so perfect. Zenze pointed in the direction away from the leopard and whispered, "we are safe while he is eating, but I don't want to wait to find out. Move everyone!"

Jamie, stunned, could not make his legs move. Temba pushed him forward and he whispered "is it, is it?" She did not answer but a knot as tight as a vice tightened itself around her chest. It cannot be Xixi, it just cannot be Xixi, she thought. Jamie kept looking over his shoulder but Temba prodded him to move along. All thoughts of danger forgotten, all he could think of was his monkey-friend Xixi. Jamie had never felt such a loss. He wanted to cry out loud and call for his friend, but the leopard was too near. He could actually hear the eating, slurping, crunching sounds the leopard was making. He felt nauseous and dizzy but the firm hand of Temba on his back made him put one foot in front of the other. Salty, stingy tears flowed down his cheeks but he could not stifle the soundless sobs that started from way inside his body. He trembled and stumbled and at one stage his mind just shut down and he couldn't think anymore. They walked in silence for what seemed like a time without end, until the sound of the waterfall was so loud they could hear nothing else.

Jamie didn't see the huge python snake wrapped around a branch just a few centimeters above his head, nor the beautifully colored butterflies flitting from one forest orchid to the other. He didn't hear the rustling of a leveret, a baby hare, as it ran away to find a new hiding place. Jamie was in another space, grieving for his monkey.

Jamie walked clutching his stomach, shoulders drooped.

Zenze moved towards an outcrop of rocks and stopped under a overhang where they were a little protected from the continual drizzle. Jamie, hunched on the ground, finally allowed his sobs to erupt from his body. Zenze touched him on his head and left him alone, sitting on his haunches a little distance away. Nelson sat with Zenze, wordlessly looking at Jamie. Temba sat with legs outstretched, back against the rock and put her hand on Jamie's shoulder. He sobbed and sobbed, at times gasping for breath. Gerbi, very alarmed at the noises, ran up Jamie's arm and sitting on his shoulder tried to lick the salty tears. Just when the children thought he had cried himself out, his sobs quieting down, he started again.

A troupe of Samango monkeys, who rarely leave the tree tops, came to see these intruders, their monkey noises making everyone look hopefully into the trees, but there was no Xixi, which made Jamie start crying all over again. "We need to move away from this drizzle to somewhere dry. I need to look at the belt again," voiced Zenze. He looked intently at the belt and said, "follow me" and with that he moved back into the dense forest, Jamie listlessly getting to his feet. Temba said, "maybe it wasn't Xixi, maybe he has joined a troupe which would be a good thing, wouldn't it Jamie?" She was trying to find something for him to cling to. He looked at Temba and opened his mouth to say something but he had cried so much he had lost his voice. They walked in silence, the drizzle diminishing until it was just a thin mist. After a long time, Zenze who was up ahead made beckoning waves with his arms and a landscape of such wonder opened up before them that even Jamie's tired brain acknowledged it.

Zenze was standing at the edge of a precipice. Far below, the raging river pounded against rocks and tugged at the roots of trees growing close to its edge. A rainbow stretched across the ravine its colors bright against the background of an enormously high waterfall. The sheer power and noise of the waterfall left the children awestruck, a little afraid and feeling small. Zenze pointed to his feet and made a slipping action to warn them against going too close to the edge. A little slip here, and they would fall into the river far below with no hope of surviving. They gazed for a while then gingerly made their way down river, following a well-worn track. They kept on taking short breaks just to look back at the waterfall and the rainbow.

As they walked further away from the waterfall, the sound became quieter until they could actually hear each other speak. They turned a bend and the world was no longer a noisy place, but a quiet haven, a place to rest. The cataracts, the rushing water in between two mountain sides, had given place to a quiet, fast moving river, smooth and peaceful with inlets here and there. In the very far distance the first sight of other humans. Women carrying bundles of washing on their heads moving away from the river and children laughing.

"Move away from the edge of the river, I don't want us to be seen," said Zenze, as he moved away. Only Jamie remained staring at the children playing on the banks of the river. A lone monkey, hanging by its tail, then dropping to the ground doing somersaults, was entertaining the children. He held his breath as he peered intently. The monkey seemed to look directly at Jamie and then disappeared into the undergrowth. Jamie turned and followed his friends silently, he could not let go of this terrible feeling of loss he was feeling. No monkey would ever replace Xixi.

Nelson and Temba had collected berries along the way and as soon as they were far enough from the children and women, they sat to eat. Again Jamie wept silent tears as he fed Gerbi berries remembering how Xixi loved them. Zenze had the belt in his hands and he and Nelson were discussing what they should do next.

"This volcano has me confused. There is a line of beads, from the tip of the mountain to a long white band of something, but we are far from the mountain. I think the white band could be that waterfall we have just seen but how can we possibly cross that raging river? Do you think those women came from Wakiri's kraal. Do you think we are this near? What about this lake that Shaka said he had seen once long ago. The one with the beautiful pink flamingo birds? I hope we are moving in the right direction."

"Have you noticed" said Nelson, "that we have been walking in a circle? We left the waterfall where the noise was so loud we could not hear each other speak, we turned a corner following the river where the sound was less ,and now, the sound of the waterfall is becoming louder with every step we take. It is either another waterfall or we are being led back to the first waterfall. I think the waterfall is important so we'll follow this track and see where it leads us."

"Do you think Jamie will ever get over what happened to Xixi? Nelson asked Zenze. "I feel so sorry for him. He loved Xixi more than anything in the world. Xixi has been Mfana's comfort ever since we found him."

Zenze answered, "to lose someone that you love must be the worst feeling possible, but with time I'm sure he will feel better. I don't think he will ever forget Xixi. Time heals but your heart never forgets. Death and loss are part of life, especially in the wild."

Zenze moved away from the children and they followed him, wiping their hands on the tall grass to get rid of the sticky berry juice. They walked in single file, Jamie bringing up the rear, dragging his feet. The sound of the waterfall became louder, the foliage thicker and the air dense with moisture. "I think we'll stop for the night," said Zenze. Nelson and Jamie set out to cut leaves from the tree ferns and dragged them to the campsite where they helped Zenze make a shelter. Temba had collected dry twigs and branches along the way and balanced them on her head as did her mother and grandmother before her. She started a fire immediately and the boys constructed the canopy over it. The box of matches Jamie had found in his box was their most prized possession.

Nelson took a hare that he had speared earlier in the day out of his pouch and began cleaning it. He skinned it expertly, put the entrails and skin into a hole and covered them with a stone. He did not want any unwelcome scavengers into their camp. He cut the hare into pieces and with a stick through each piece, handed one to each friend. They huddled together around the fire holding the pieces of hare over the flames, until the smell of cooking meat made their stomachs rumble with hunger. There was no bantering. There was no teasing. The two loeries in the trees were squabbling over a good perch for the night. An owl screeched, perhaps it had seen a mouse for its dinner. Far in the distance they heard a leopard cough and Jamie's eyes widened in terror while his whole body trembled. He felt for the furry comfort of Gerbi in his pocket. They looked around into the intense darkness and a few pairs of yellow eyes looked back at them and then moved away, afraid of the fire. The night animals were out on the prowl and darkness was closing in on them.

As their clothes dried on them from the heat of the fire, and they silently ate, licking their fingers, they began to feel sleepy. Zenze offered to take the first watch to keep the fire burning throughout the night and Nelson would take the next. One by one they curled up next to each other and fell asleep.

Zenze fingered the beaded belt and let his thoughts travel to his father's words:

Shaka recalled, "I was a very young boy, like you, and so afraid of initiation. I know the place of initiation was close to Wakiri's kraal. Horrifendi the witchdoctor was in charge of us and he made the experience as terrifying as possible. Should you find the kraal, be wary of him. He will poison Wakiri's thoughts and make things as difficult as possible for you, especially as you are my son."

Zenze felt they were close to the kraal but wondered where the entrance could be. He knew the clue to the secret entrance to the village was somewhere beaded in the belt. He had heard that it was guarded by fierce warriors and strange wild animals, but that could have been just to keep strangers away. He wondered what they would find at the kraal. Would Temba's mother welcome them? Would Wakiri be kind to them? Would Horrifendi cast a spell on them? What or who had been following them? Would there be any good news for Jamie?

He looked up at the black sky dotted with thousands of stars and wondered what they were. Sometimes the old people used to say the stars were ancestors looking down on earth. He wondered and wondered as he stoked the fire, making sure it burned. Soon it was time for Nelson to take the shift and Zenze too curled next to his friends and fell asleep.

Temba had taken the shift just before dawn and she too kept thinking of her mother and how she had beaded the belt and made all those necklaces and bracelets for her to keep her memory alive. She understood how each bead must have been a bead of love. Seeing Jamie's sorrow at the loss of his monkey, she thought of the sorrow her own mother must have felt when she had to say goodbye to her little girl. How could she have survived? Temba became more convinced that her mother would do everything she could do to help her. She was still too young to get married. She said a silent 'thank you' to Refilwe and Shaka, her aunt and uncle, who had looked after her and loved her more than she could ever repay, and had encouraged her to speak her thoughts openly. Shaka kept telling her that times were changing and it was right for girls to have a say in their future.

The sky changed from a dark black to an indigo blue, then orange-yellow and finally the sun made its appearance. Temba boiled some water in the three legged pot and started to prepare porridge for breakfast. Jamie, always the last, was first to appear, looking bedraggled with black rings under his eyes, slumped to the ground around the fire. No sooner had he sat down than he lay on the ground, arms and legs flailing. Temba let out a scream, 'aiee, aiee' that made the boys jump up out of their sleep, grab their knives and look for the wild animal that was attacking the group. Temba, ran to hide behind a tree. Jamie was doing a wild dance, his mouth open in a soundless scream with a monkey clinging to his back. Xixi had returned, safe and sound.

CHAPTER 25

The pink beads in the belt

he forest reverberated with clapping of hands, stamping of feet and such loud happy laughter that some yellow *weaver* birds just waking up to the morning flew in confused disorder from branch to branch, their bell-like nests swaying in the breeze.

A troupe of monkeys that had followed Xixi screeched loudly and swung on vines from tree to tree. The two loerie birds flapped their wings loudly and entangled themselves in some vines, squawking 'kay-waaay kay-waay'.

Jamie could not stop hugging Xixi who opened his mouth wide and stuck his tongue out in pleasure. He snapped his teeth together and chattered non-stop. Zenze, Nelson and Temba alternately just stared

or patted the monkey and tried to hug Jamie at the same time. At one stage, Jamie jumping around crazily turned his head just as Zenze was bending down to pat Xixi, bumped Zenze's mouth with his head and chipped Zenze's top tooth. Blood seeped out of Zenze's mouth but no one noticed until much later, they were all so excited at Xixi's return.

Jamie, still voiceless, shook his head a hundred times. "How?, where?," were the words bandied around by the children. It was a while before Temba could serve the porridge and no food had ever tasted as good as what they ate that morning. Xixi and Gerbi shared their porridge and at last Jamie could be seen smiling again, in fact that grin stayed on his face for a long time.

They cleaned up camp and moved along the edge of the river at quite a steep incline, the path interweaving in and out of the thick bush. Berries grew in profusion and they stopped frequently to gorge on them. Nelson was the expert on berries and no one ate a berry without asking him whether it was poisonous or not. The children were taught from a young age that some berries were poisonous and could cause death.

Xixi did not stray from Jamie for a moment, in fact he kept on pulling him forwards. If only Xixi could talk! The children wanted to know: How had he crossed the river? Why had he run away from them? Where had he been for such a long time?

The sound of the waterfall was again muffled as the track took a sharp turn to the right and dropped even further down. The group, as one, exclaimed "ooh! and aah!' at the sight before them.

A huge lake, with an island, in the middle of a lake, so big they could not see the other side, appeared before them. Its blue water so translucent that the point where it joined the skyline could barely be seen. The island looked like a pink, moving blur. What the children were staring at was a mass of pink flamingos (see p.187). Thousands and thousands of loud honking, long, pink-legged, white and pink birds. Some were wading in the water, long necks submerged underwater looking for food, others grooming themselves, twisting their long necks to reach under wings and far parts of their bodies. Some, standing on one leg, flapped their wings to catch the sun or to ready themselves for flight. The sight of this huge number of birds with pink and white feathers was so beautiful that the children were speechless. At some unknown signal a large part of the flock took off in flight and the bright red spots of their forewings looked like flames in the sky. Temba held her hands over her heart and said "I have never seen anything so beautiful in my whole life".

Jamie, holding Xixi's hand just nodded, he still had no voice Again the glimmer of a tear, a happy tear, glistened on his cheek. When he had woken up, after the aeroplane accident, he could not remember anything, so his sense of loss had not been too severe, but now, with the experience of thinking he had lost Xixi to the leopard, the floodgates of loss overwhelmed him. He longed to know about his parents. He longed to know about his previous life. He longed with such an intensity he felt as if he had a tight fist just under his ribs. He so hoped he would find answers to his questions at the end of this journey.

The children found a shady spot to sit and admire the flamingo birds, trying to grasp the beauty unfolding before their eyes. Gerbi found some rocks and scampered around, darting in, out and around them, scratching in the ground looking for something to eat. Jamie held fast to the little cord around his friend and threw him some berries which Xixi surreptitiously stole one at a time.

Temba fingered her belt and rubbed the pink part, feeling very close to her mother. "Mama I'm here, I feel

I am close to you." Xixi took Jamie's hand and jumping up and down, clapping his teeth pulled him to his feet. "I think he wants to show me something." Zenze stretched to his feet and started moving and then, turning to Jamie said "I think you and Xixi should lead for a while. If you are ahead of me, I can keep an eye on you two."

Xixi became more agitated as they walked until they were so close to the waterfall that again they were drenched to the skin and walking became slippery and dangerous. At one stage Temba refused to walk any further, she sat down in a sulk. "If we are to keep following Xixi he'll have us climbing up the waterfall's rock face and I just cannot do that – we'll hurt ourselves. For goodness sakes, he thinks we are monkeys like him!"

Jamie signed to her to wait and then made walking movements with his fingers while pointing to himself and Xixi. Zenze nodded and they watched him move away. Jamie walked a few steps and then seemed to hesitate. He turned back, giving Gerbi to Temba. She understood what a great gesture that was. She knew that there were times in life where one knows to let go. It is part of growing up.

Xixi pulled Jamie, who by this time was hanging onto anything he could get a hold of. The rocks covered in lichen were slimy, the plants on the ground equally slippery. Jamie thought that at any moment he would slip and be dashed on the rocks below. They were not following any visible path and Jamie tugged at Xixi's hand but the monkey ignored him and pulled him behind a huge rock. They skirted the rock and to Jamie's utter amazement he found himself on a path that led behind the waterfall. The noise was very, very loud and Xixi scampered ahead then disappeared. Jamie's heart lurched. ' Oh no!, not again!' he thought, but a small monkey face peeked at him from behind a rock.

Jamie lost concentration for a moment and the ground beneath him gave way. He clutched at a root, but his grip slipped, he clung to a vine but his feet could not find a hold and he hung suspended above the water. As he looked up, unable to call out he saw the most horrendous face. A huge purple face with sharp pointed rotting teeth. Green slime dripping from its jaws falling into the water below, causing the water to turn into bubbling mud. Its hair a mass of undulating snakes that hissed and tried to strike Jamie. The vision divided into many monsters, all more hideous than the first, all trying to attack Jamie. He had no voice, the others could not hear him, his arms felt as if they would be torn out of their sockets. He let out a soundless cry, "mommy help" and in that instant Xixi belted into him and hung around his neck. Xixi had swung towards Jamie on a vine and the momentum pushed his feet against the side of the mountain. He clung to a root but his grip was weak, his arm and shoulder muscles screaming with pain. When he thought he could hold on no longer, two pairs of hands grabbed him. Nelson and Zenze helped him and Xixi up the slippery mountain side.

Zenze was so relieved that Jamie had not fallen to his death on the rocks below that he did not take much notice of what he was trying to tell him with his hands. Jamie wanted to tell Zenze about the monster and even though he made terrible faces with fingers in his mouth, stretching his lips and pulling down his bottom eye lids, Zenze did not understand, he just shook his head. Jamie glanced down the precipice to the river and saw what looked like boiling water, but it was a vivid green whirlpool sucking the remains of the monsters. He turned around to tell someone but there was no one to tell, besides he had no voice. He looked down again, but there was nothing, only a sense of peace. Had he actually seen anything? Was it his imagination? Xixi was again pulling Jamie by the hand and as they walked around the rock, the children looked in amazement at the path behind the waterfall. The path was wet but not slippery and about halfway behind the waterfall curtain, an opening yawned in the rock leading to a tunnel with a light at the end of it. The entrance, the secret entrance. Yes it had to be.

The four children could not believe the strange feeling of being behind the waterfall – what a wonderful camouflage for an entrance. They all touched the rock face and washed their faces with the spray from the waterfall but no one made a move to enter the tunnel, it was as if they were afraid of what awaited them on the other side. If this was the entrance to Wakiri's kraal, where were the fierce warriors they had heard of? Why was no one guarding the entrance?

Finally, Jamie holding Xixi by the hand made a move and Nelson touched him on his shoulder and gave him a high five. It was time for Nelson to go back to let the family know they had found the entrance – he was sure of it. Now he understood the message of the beads in the last square of the belt. The brown mass of beads with a thin strip of blue and white beads was the waterfall falling down the mountain.

CHAPTER 26

...does the boy speak?

ixi ran ahead and the three friends cautiously exited the tunnel, each one expecting the worst. Nothing happened. Nothing stirred, just lush vegetation and a smell of cooking fires. A well trodden path led them downwards, turning this way and that until as if by magic an entire kraal lay before them with people going about their business. Out of nowhere came a flurry of little children laughing and making loud noises. Xixi ran into Jamie's arms and Gerbi, who had been sitting on Jamie's shoulder, crept inside his shirt, just the little cord showing. The kraal children circled the little group and led them forwards. Temba's eyes darted every which way, because by now the adults had been alerted and were turning to look at the cause of the noise. Some women came out of huts, wiping their hands on hips or an apron. Some stopped stoking the fires to look at a very unusual sight.

Some men, sitting in the shade smoking a pipe stood and walked towards them.

As if they were a magnet, the people of the kraal moved towards them. They were led to a central area where an old man sat under a tree, surrounded by many women and children. The leopard skin on his shoulders showed he was obviously the chief. The children were most intrigued with Jamie, never having seen a white child before and they touched him, especially his hair, then pulled away shrieking with glee.

Temba stepped forward, touching her left side where her heart lived and bent her head to the Chief. "I am Temba, daughter of Ntsepe. My friends and I are looking for the kraal of Chief Wakiri."

"Welcome, daughter of Ntsepe, you have found us. We are your family."

"This is Zenze my cousin and this is Jamie who is looking for his parents."

"We had heard that a group of children were seen near the sacred stones, but we did not know who you were. Horrifendi died sometime ago, but his spirit has been wandering around the forest, unable to give up life in this world and we have not ventured out of the village for fear of his evil. Did you perhaps encounter his spirit?"

asked Wakiri. Zenze and Temba looked at each other with a knowing look, but said nothing.

Just then, high-pitched singing and loud ululating voices were heard. Dozens of women and children moved towards the chief's shelter. The women ran from their huts, their beaded ankles making a sound like pebbles rubbing together. A woman, adjusting her headdress, almost stumbling in her haste, ran towards Temba with arms outstretched crying, "Temba, it is I, Ntsepe, your mother." Without hesitation Temba ran into those arms she had missed for so long and between kisses, crying, and hugs forgot the world for a while.

Addressing Zenze, Wakiri asked, "does this white boy speak.? Does he understand us?"

"He does speak, sometimes too much," he said with a wry smile. " He speaks not only our language but his own as well. He has lost his voice, but I am sure he will soon recover it. We have reason to believe that his mother is alive and living in this kraal."

Jamie had scanned all the faces around him and with a sinking heart had not seen one that could be his mother.

"You have been sent to us at a very important time. As I said before, Horrifendi passed into the spirit world a full moon ago and tomorrow we are to celebrate the naming of his successor. We are to have a huge feast and you will be part of it. Come and tell me the story of this white boy."

Zenze sat down at Wakiri's feet and said, "before I tell you Mfana's story, please answer one question – why were there no guards to the entrance, how were we able to walk straight into your village?" Wakiri smiled, and said that it was Horrifendi and his followers who had guarded the entrance and now that he was no longer with them, they had left the entrance unguarded to welcome anyone who wanted to visit.

Zenze gave a shudder and wondered whether it had been Horrifendi's spirit that had followed them. Had it been the witchdoctor's last attempt at upsetting Temba's wish? Or was it something else? He gathered his thoughts and began to tell Jamie's story. While he spoke, many young boys and girls gathered around him to hear him better. His eyes kept on straying to one particular pretty girl. She sat at Wakiri's right hand and he at times placed a tender hand on her head. At one point in the story, he turned to her and smilingly said, "Iza, please bring your old father and these fine young men something to drink." Jamie listened to Zenze tell his story and occasionally nodded his head.

Dark clouds were gathering and in the distance while lightening streaked the sky. Thunder rumbled ominously. Wakiri looked expectantly at the sky - they had been waiting for the rains for a long time. Water in Africa is so scarce, so precious. Zenze paused in his story-telling for a moment to look at the sky and take a sip of his drink when the first large drops of rain began to fall. A loud, joyous ululating sound enveloped the kraal. The children laughingly ran in the rain, turning their mouths up to the sky to catch a delicious drop. The smaller children stomped in the mud pools feeling the coolness between their toes, oblivious of the mud spatter that covered their bodies.

"You have brought us good luck" said Wakiri. "you have brought us rain." Now you must rest and tomorrow you can continue your story. Iza led them to Ntsepe's hut where Temba sat in the doorway, the belt draped across her lap – a smile as wide as a river on her face.

"Jamie, Zenze did you see my mother? Is she not beautiful? She has gone to bring us some food. Oh! I am so happy!" babbled Temba, then looking at Jamie, her expression changed to one of concern, "Jamie, your mother?" Jamie hung his head and shook it. Temba felt selfish, she had been so overjoyed at seeing her mother that she had forgotten Jamie. An endless stream of men, women and children converged on Ntsepe's thatched hut to either bring food, chat or just stare. There were some members of the tribe who had never been out of the village. While Horrifendi was alive, he controlled the villagers with threats of pain, vengeance and fear and told false tales of the horrors that lived outside the village. Wakiri had not known this until the old man who helped the medicine lady told him.

Temba was touched, admired, hugged by so many well-wishers that later she could not remember anyone in particular. She did however remember that Ntsepe had said that her father had died and now Ntsepe was head of her family and could decide for Temba.

Zenze played the young warrior, a little detached and aloof. With dignity, he accepted all the praise for leading Temba back to her mother safely. Temba thought he was puffing his chest out a little too much, but was so busy greeting people she let it go. As the leader, he was feted by the young girls, especially Iza, and treated with respect by the other young boys his age. Zenze casually asked where Drako was, and was told he was out hunting. Zenze silently repeated "one day, one day" to himself.

Jamie felt so disappointed and lonely in the midst of

this mass of people, he looked for Xixi's comfort but could not see him. He looked towards a cluster of children throwing stones at something in a tree and his heart lurched – it was Xixi. In a red mist of rage, he ran to the tree and with arms flailing and much shaking of his head he angrily faced the children with a hard and unwavering stare. He held his arms out to Xixi and walked towards the hut with him. Wakiri had seen how Jamie had faced the naughty children and smiled. Here was a true warrior, not only did he have the quality of courage but also kindness to animals. He had seen these true warrior qualities in Jamie and was pleased. He would scold the children later, as he would not tolerate cruelty to animals in his kraal.

At some time during the evening, when Ntsepe had begged the villagers to go back to their own huts so the children could sleep, the children curled up in blankets and fell into a deep sleep immediately. Xixi in between Jamie and Zenze with Gerbi neatly tucked into Jamie's neck, rounded tummy evidence of all the seeds he had been plied with during the day.

It was still very dark, the sky a deep indigo, mist covered the huts like a cloak and eerie shadows turned every object into a heaving mass, when a figure approached Ntsepe's hut. Two taps on the outer wall woke Zenze.

"Wake up the white boy, you and he are to leave now to go and find his mother." said Wakiri. Jamie was already out of the blankets, tucking Gerbi into his pocket.

"You need to go now, before the rest of the village wakes. I want you back this evening for the festivities. Take the path behind the goat corral, it will take you through a forest of baobab trees. Look for the biggest one and go through it. Go, don't ask any questions, just go," ordered Wakiri.

Zenze and Jamie slunk out of the hut, Xixi tightly gripping Jamie's hand. Zenze beckoned Jamie and put his finger over his lips. They walked in this liquid landscape, their thoughts unspooling like threads. Jamie wanted to ask Zenze questions, but that same finger across the lips was his answer. They smelt the goats before they heard their bleating. They entered the baobab forest in the quiet, tranquil time, just before sunrise, when the cool red earth of Africa meets the grey gentle breeze. They could almost taste the sunrise.

Zenze at last said, we need to look for the largest tree." Jamie lifted his eyebrows in a silent 'why'?

"We are going to find your mother". Jamie stopped in his tracks, his eyes wide with disbelief. As if a surge of power had overtaken him, he started running from one tree to the other, looking up into the branches to judge which would be the largest. What did Wakiri mean by 'the largest.' The tallest, the widest the oldest? He was caught in the grip of fear that they would not be able to find it.

One huge tree, tucked well up against a hill caught his eye and Jamie headed for it. Wakiri had said "go through it". The forest, the tree? – impossible.

Xixi had joined in the frenzy and ran up one tree after the other, gibbering non-stop and calling 'xi,xi'. Jamie circled the tree and gave a gasp. Snuggled right up between the rock face and the baobab was a camouflaged opening. He gave the mousebird call for Zenze and plunged in. A vista of great beauty unfolded before him. He had entered an old volcano crater filled with flowers, herbs and plants of every description. Not a breath of air ruffled the plants and a perfume so strong it almost took his breath away, wafted over him. In the distance, bending over a clump of brilliant yellow flowers stood a figure. Jamie shielded his eyes against the rising sun and as he did so, she turned to face him. It was the lady with the golden hair. His knees buckled causing him to kneel amongst the plants. As if in slow motion he watched her start moving towards him, first just walking, then running until finally her arms were

271

around him. He tasted her tears mingled with his before he uttered his first word in many days, " MOM."

Zenze stopped in his tracks when he saw the two figures hugging each other, smiled and turned around. He was so happy he jumped up and down and did a little warrior's dance all on his own. He looked back once and saw Xixi running around in circles, he was so excited.

Jamie's mom took him to a little hut where she lived and gave him some special brew. She did not take her eyes off him for a second, perhaps afraid that he would disappear into thin air if she blinked her eyes. She spoke in a language half English and half African, and so did he. She held both his hands in hers and sitting in front of him began. "I have never stopped hoping that you were alive. The plane crash. We were shot at by bad men who wanted to know about the diamond mines your dad was going to work in. Your dad was a good man, he wanted to stop the illegal trade in blood diamonds.

"My dad? Where is my dad?" whispered Jamie, his voice coming back little by little.

His mom shook her head sadly and said, "he is dead, he died in the crash"

"Jamie held his mom's hands and said, "we found the box. We found the stones and lots of other things"

"How wonderful, I have use for some of the medicines in it.. Did you find the map?"

"What's a map? Is it a rolled up piece of paper? We found something like that but didn't know what it was."

His mom clapped her hands with happiness. "We will talk about all of these things later, now I just want to see you and make sure you are really here."

"But mom, how did you come to this kraal?"

"The bad men brought me all tied up to Wakiri's kraal because they had no use for a white woman and Horrifendi thought I might be able to help with the women in the kraal. Horrifendi was a wicked man, keeping me secreted and forbidding me to leave the village, with threats that he would find you if you were alive and kill you. I was never able to speak to Wakiri directly, but Ntsepe helped me and we were planning a trip to come and find you, now that Horrifendi is dead. I cannot believe my eyes that you are here with me. I have so many questions." Jamie just stroked her cheeks and could not stop the tears that were rolling down his face. "You are the golden lady of my dreams, you have always been with me, I just didn't know you." Jamie's mom started to laugh when a furry monkey, caught up in the moment leapt into her lap and smothered her with monkey kisses.

GLOSSARY OF TERMS

biltong	dried strips of meat
gogo	grandmother
isigquolo	container for crushing corn
isiqcawa	meeting place
kraal	village
llanga	sun
lobola	bride price
marogo	wild spinach
mfana	little boy
miggies	species of small flies
mntwana	little girl
mopane worms	species of caterpillar
muti	medicine
pap	cooked white corn meal
potjie pot	Three legged cooking pot
skokiaan	tribal brew
tokoloshe (tiki)	mischievous spirit

Printed in Great Britain
by Amazon